Out of Time

Out of Time

Also by Bruce Macfarlane

Science Fiction
A Drift Out of Time
A House Out of Time
The Space Between Time
Three Tales Out of Time
The Webs of Time

History
Notes on Arthurian Literature

Out of Time

The first book from
The Time Travel Diaries of
James Urquhart and Elizabeth Bicester

by
Bruce Macfarlane

2nd Edition

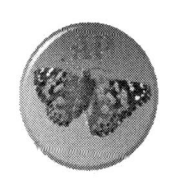

Aldwick Publishing

Out of Time

Copyright © 2018 Bruce Macfarlane
Aldwick Publishing
www.aldwickpublishing.com
All rights reserved.

ISBN-13: 978-1-9164024-1-6

Out of Time

DEDICATION

For
Julia, Heather and Alan
Whom I love very much.

Out of Time

Preface

Welcome to the time travel diaries of James Urquhart, 21st century minor science lecturer, and his Victorian companion Elizabeth Bicester, as narrated by Professor Rolleston.

The reader may find the format of the Time Travel Diaries unusual. They are written in the form of an epistolary novel whereby the diaries of the two main characters, Elizabeth and James, are combined in chronological order (or as much as they can be in a time travel novel).

The reason for this was simple. I wanted the hero and heroine to present their adventures from their own perspectives. To do this, I decided that Prof. Rolleston edits the diaries so that first one character and then the other relates events as they happened, and in their own words.

I hope that makes sense and that you enjoy the story.

Author: Bruce Macfarlane, February 2019

Out of Time

Out of Time

Acknowledgements

Julia Macfarlane & Heather Robbins – Editing.

Images & Illustrations.
Art work by author using PicsArt Photo Studio for Android and PaintShop Pro.
Cover: The Orloj, Prague with PicsArt and Paint Shop Pro
Chapter 1: Cricket, Sussex Village. Author's photo
Chapter 2: As Cover with Photo of Moon taken with Author's Celestron C8 Telescope
Chapter 3: Author's photo. Living room
Chapter 4: Author's photos. Submarine, Barcelona. Background: Asturias.
Chapter 6: Maxwell's Field Equations
Chapter 7: Author's Photo: house
Chapter 8: Author's Photo: Palmerston Fort Tunnel.
Chapter 9: Author's Photo: Odds and Ends in Garage.
Chapter 10: As Cover.
Chapter 11: Author's photo: Old electronic board.
Part III: Author's photo of Moon and Sunset.
Chapter 12: Author's "attic"
Chapter 13: Author's photos: Moon and Cathedral.
Chapter 14: Author's photos: old electronic board.
Chapter 15: Author's photos: Collage: Submarine, Barcelona & Steam train on North Yorkshire Moors Railway.
Chapter 16: Author's photo of cathedral.
Chapter 17: Author's photo: Kingley Vale, West Sussex.
Star fields in images: Star-Forming Region LH 95 in the Large Magellanic Cloud: Credit: NASA/ESA. https://upload.wikimedia.org/wikipedia/commons/8/87/LH_95.jpg

Out of Time

Introduction

Trying to socially engineer the world's population is not easy, especially when you discover that a pair of reluctant time travellers keep on getting in the way of your plan.

The problems started when James Urquhart, living in 2015, was enjoying a walk in the countryside and stumbled upon Elizabeth Bicester at a cricket match at Hamgreen in 1873.

If only Time would stay where it is, it would be a lot easier for everyone.

Here is the first volume of the time travel diaries, narrated by Professor Rolleston, of the humorous and sometimes romantic adventures of James Urquhart, minor science lecturer living in 2015 and Elizabeth Bicester, whom he stumbled upon at a cricket match at Hamgreen in 1873.

Somehow, despite their banter regarding each other's manners and background they manage through incredible feats of illogical deduction and with not a little help from James Maxwell, H. G. Wells, the Martians and some strange time devices, to save the world.

Out of Time

Table of Contents

- Preface vii
- Acknowledgements ix
- Introduction xi
- Prologue 1
- Part I A Game of Cricket 7
- Chapter One 9
- Chapter Two 30
- Chapter Three 48
- Chapter Four 73
- Chapter Five 90
- Chapter Six 98
- Chapter Seven 106
- Comment by Professor Rolleston 113
- Part II Down the Rabbit Hole 115
- Chapter Eight 116
- Chapter Nine 122
- Chapter Ten 143
- Chapter Eleven 153
- A Letter from Mr Wells 169
- Part III The Martians 171
- Prologue 173
- Chapter Twelve 177
- Chapter Thirteen 188
- Chapter Fourteen 196
- Chapter Fifteen 209
- Chapter Sixteen 218
- Chapter Seventeen 228
- Other Books by Bruce Macfarlane 243
- About the Author 246

Out of Time

Out of Time

Prologue

ComsMesh

The First Phase

In 2021CE the Weber Institute activated its darknet site ComsMesh to access and hack into the world's government, social and financial services' personal data banks. At the same time it bought out two major social media sites and, under the umbrella of its media vehicle Adcom, channelled their subscribers' personal data through a darknet conduit to ComsMesh. The Weber Institute then meshed subscribers' social media data with their personal data banks and uploaded it to Adcom, which used the data to accurately match products with subscribers' needs.

Within a year most suppliers and vendors had no alternative but to sign up to Adcom's product placement services due to Adcom's phenomenal ability to target and match product to subscribers.

As most Adcom subscribers were hooked on their social media sites for communication, to further encourage product purchase a time lapse between purchases was introduced which if exceeded would remove the subscriber from Adcom. This was initially one month but within three years this had been reduced to eight hours. To help subscribers keep signed on, apps were created by the Weber Institute which could be downloaded and would regularly poll Adcom and purchase small, cheap or free items such as travel coupons, book chapters or games based on the person's profile extracted from ComsMesh data banks. So that subscribers felt they were in control, the apps allowed users to set monetary limits on individual purchases. However, by the manipulative use of 'tasters' and posting of 'satisfied' customers who had increased their limits to receive more interesting purchases, subscribers also began to increase their limits.

These apps were extremely popular as they supplied the users with what they hadn't realised they wanted but unfortunately at the same time whittled away at their finances. To keep people buying the Weber Institute initially created a range of loan companies such as CashCom to help finance users' purchases. However, even ComsMesh realised that there was only a limited amount of real and imaginary money to go around.

The Second Phase

The breakthrough came when Dr Anderson of the Weber Institute realised that there was actually no need for money and devised a social structure program that if kept in equilibrium would lock suppliers and subscribers into a permanent hold.

Anderson had realised that by this time most subscribers were so happy with the items Adcom purchased for them that very few people were now actually consciously buying products on their own. It was therefore a relatively simple matter to remove subscribers' rights to decide what to purchase and allow Adcom to supply what they needed without purchase. This was implemented under ComsMesh Directive No. 1. The Weber Institute and ComsMesh now had total influence and control over an individual's decision making.

Product placement now matched the subscribers'

unconscious wants and desires with availability; however, for complete control ComsMesh needed expertise in product placement that could be used to manipulate or change the subscriber's profile and direct them to other products which then could be used to further influence and manipulate subscribers. To facilitate this the Weber Institute's Department of Structural Social Engineering devised algorithms to test manipulation on sample subscribers. These tests were found to be a complete success and under ComsMesh Directive No. 2 the algorithms were applied to all Adcom subscribers.

The Third Phase

Now with complete control of AdCom subscribers, the Weber Institute approached the United Nations Security Council and offered to provide a socially engineered methodology whereby governments, using the expertise and facilities of the Weber Institute, could create ordered societies that matched their needs.

In a world with over ten billion people and rapidly diminishing resources this offer was taken up with enthusiasm

----

Addendum to the Report on the Diaries of James Urquhart and Elizabeth Bicester

Submitted by Professor Rolleston,
Dept. of Social & Cultural Engineering,
Weber Institute,
Mons Olympus,
Mars.

As is well known to those of you who subscribe to my ComsMesh media feed, the diaries were found clasped and bound together in a copper chest in the attic of a Lodge at Hamgreen in Sussex. They purport to be the diaries of a James Urquhart and an Elizabeth Bicester written in the year 2015 CE. The one of James Urquhart is written in an undisciplined style using a ball stylus in a thick ruled black notebook, and the other by nib and ink and also ball stylus in an ornate leather-bound tooled diary and written in copperplate.

Both diaries describe the same extraordinary events and seem to be written in unison. Until recently they were thought to be a collaborative fictional adventure or part of an elaborate hoax whose purpose is still unknown. However, chemical and ocular analysis by John Frobisher at Manchester University has now shown that the paper and inks of the two diaries are technologically separated by over a hundred years and therefore could not have been written at the same time.

If only one or the other existed then the story could be dismissed as a fabrication but the existence of both with what I now believe to be almost seamless correlation between them, as I hope to show in my narrative, has led me to the almost impossible conclusion that both persons were able to perform time dimensional travel.

The implications of this are profound. The possible existence of movement through time would provide a degree of freedom that cannot be controlled by the Institute's algorithms and would allow Adcom subscribers to know in advance products assigned to them and to others.

Such future knowledge could raise the level of consciousness of subscribers leading again to uncontrolled freedom of thought and individual decision making. It is therefore imperative that my conclusion that time movement exists is tested and I propose that initially subscribers' historical purchasing databases are examined to determine whether any purchases have deviated from the constraints of the algorithms. Such deviations would indicate that time travel exists and more importantly identify the individuals involved.

My transcription of the two diaries into one narrative is designed to test the story's consistency and to determine whether they were a joint enterprise or both taken independently possibly from another as yet unknown diary. For the sake of brevity and to try to improve the narrative flow I have where possible removed duplication of events, and where meetings between the two persons overlap I have created dialogues based on the texts and attempted to use their own vernacular.

I have also taken the liberty of giving this narrative a title of 'Out of Time' and used the letter J for Urquhart and E for Bicester to distinguish from which diary the narrative is derived. Those of you who wish to compare my interpretation with the original texts are referred to J. Stonewell's well-known thesis 'The Urquhart-Bicester Diaries'

Out of Time

Part I A Game of Cricket

Out of Time

Chapter One

J.

It had been a nice morning. We had walked about four and a half miles and it was approaching lunchtime. White cotton wool clouds were beginning to rise and roll over the Downs and the beech trees were starting to show their iridescent green leaves against their darkened boughs.

Just as we were emerging from a copse I spotted in the undergrowth an orange tip land near some honey fungus growing on the remains of an old rotting silver birch. I left the path and followed it, trying to get a good photograph with my phone, but each time I drew near it felt my shadow and danced away. Another caught my eye but when I turned I noticed my friends Mike and Peter were no longer there. I got up and quickly followed the path I thought they had taken, carefully avoiding the trailing brambles.

Suddenly I heard a loud thwack followed by a ripple of applause and turned just in time to see a cricketer swipe an excellent ball across a green into someone's garden. I still couldn't see my friends, so I decided to leave the copse and walk over to the green to get my bearings. As I emerged from the trees I felt a soft breeze blow across me and chatter though the leaves above.

By the edge of the green there was a cart decorated like one of those gypsy caravans you see in open-air museums on which sat two rather scruffy old farm hands smoking pipes and watching the game. They were enjoying quaffing a couple of tankards of beer which suddenly made me feel quite thirsty. I walked slowly over to them brushing the undergrowth off me.

"Good morning. Could you tell me what village this is,

please?"

The older one looked down at me rather sharply and said in a strong Sussex accent,

"'Tis afternoon, sir, and it be Hamgreen."

And turned back to the game.

--- ~ ---

E.

My cousin Henry had just made a mighty swipe at the ball and sent it flying into Mrs Winshall's garden again when I noticed a man talking to old Ted and Albert on the haywain. He was wearing close-fitting grey and olive-green clothes with what seemed to be a knapsack on his back. He was tall and vaguely thin but seemed to carry himself well. I noticed Ted pointed him in our direction and he started rather hesitantly to walk towards us. I turned to my sister.

"Flory, look at that man there."

"Where?"

"By the haywain."

"What outlandish clothing! He seems to be wearing some kind of poacher's outfit, Elizabeth."

"He may be looking for the shoot. Look Flory, I think he is coming towards us."

He had now composed himself but still looked a little uncertain. As he came closer I noticed that he was wearing neither hat nor shirt, just what seemed to be a soft grey-green jacket over a blue vest.

--- ~ ---

J.

I thought the best course of action was to head straight for the Cricket Club to get directions to the local pub where I hoped to meet my friends.

As I got closer it became obvious that some kind of local charity match was on as the women had donned period fancy dress and the men were wearing those schoolboy coloured caps and striped blazers which you see in those society mags of the Henley Regatta.

As I approached, two of the women sitting by a table shading themselves with parasols noticed me and started pointing and, rather disconcertingly, seemed to be quietly giggling. They obviously thought I was part of the party and had forgotten to bring my costume. I decided to ask them for directions and see where it led me. They were both dressed in what looked like fine, white, heavily embroidered, linen dresses which flowed in overlapping waves down to their ankles. Their hair was piled high in complicated ringlets on which perched small brimmed hats with what looked like fresh wild flowers in the hat bands. They had obviously gone to some effort for they reminded me of one of Tissot's paintings of idyllic young ladies.

When I reached the table I said, "Excuse me. I seem to have lost my friends."

"What do they look like?" replied one of them. Her eyes had that confidence that you sometimes see in persons used to command. But they were soft and looked as if within there might be a door through which one could enter if you had the right key.

"Well," I said, trying to keep my eyes off her eyes and her rather tight bodice, "They will look a bit like me, rather scruffy and dressed for a ramble in this wonderful countryside."

"No, we have not seen anyone dressed like you. We would have been sure to remember, wouldn't we Flory?" and with a slight giggle her eyes darted to her friend.

"Would you like some lemonade, sir?" Offered her friend.

After a morning's walking it was very easy to take up their offer and their company. My friends could wait.

---~---

E.

He seemed very at ease in our presence though I was a little surprised that he had not introduced himself. I also felt my person was receiving a little too much unwarranted attention from someone to whom I not been introduced.

"And pray tell me, what is your name, sir?"

"I'm James."

"So, Mr James, do you live locally?"

"What, oh, no my name is James Urquhart, and I do live locally. Gosh you are really staying in character, aren't you?"

I could see this was going to be a difficult; he did not seem to want to introduce himself properly to us at all. But before I could enquire further he changed the subject.

"They could be at the pub. Do you know where the local pub is?"

He talked very casually as though he was with close friends. He was quite impertinent.

"I have no idea, sir. Perhaps you can ask one of the farm hands over there."

"Great. By the way, who's winning?"

"Lord Fotheringale and his club, sir. I fear the locals will not be able to hold them off."

He smirked and slowly shook his head slowly and said, "I think I might be a little out of my class here."

"That is for you to decide, sir," I replied with a slight frown for I could not fully ascertain his background.

He looked a little perplexed at that, which drew my attention to his clothes. There were no buttons on his jacket and there was a strange embroidery on his vest like an old carriage. His hands were very white and clean so he was clearly not a working man but his boots were very heavy and covered in mud. He seemed to have walked a long way and I began to feel a little sorry for him. Perhaps he was down on his uppers. Perhaps he was hungry. I took a chance.

"May I offer you a sandwich?"

"Are you sure? Do you have enough to go around?"

"Sir, there are plenty for everyone. We have been preparing them all morning. In fact Flory and I have seen more than enough cucumbers for one week."

This provoked a strange expression of mock shock on his face, which when he saw me notice he quickly turned and rather studiously watched the cricket. I was intrigued by his manner and decided I wished to know more about him, despite convention.

"Please, sit down, Mr Urquhart. You look like you would enjoy a short rest from your travels."

---~---

J.

I sat down at the table and admired the sandwiches and cakes. All the crusts had been removed. I quickly scoffed a very delicate cucumber sandwich.

"Sir, please take a napkin or you will ruin your clothes."

I took one placed it on my lap with what I hoped was an elegant flourish, then I sat back and stretched my legs which allowed me to take a closer look at them. What I assumed to be the elder of the two was looking at me with an air of curiosity, and she held my gaze a little longer than expected.

"Well, sir …" she said.

"Please, call me James."

She looked a little alarmed then recovered and said rather seriously, "How very informal! We have not been properly introduced. Perhaps I had better tell you a little about our family and then perhaps you will be more forthcoming about your background."

Before I could recover from that she said.

"We are Elizabeth and Flory Bicester from High Lodge where our Father is Squire to Lord Fotheringale."

Were they trying to put me in my place? They could be some of the old 'Smart Set' escaped from Surrey and out to impress the natives ... Well, two can play at that game.

"And I'm James Urquhart, son of Archibald Urquhart, Lord of the Isle of Bute and 'er all that Ilk."

This provided an unintended reaction.

"Gosh, I had not realised, Sir that the Urquhart family connections extended so far. Pray tell me, how are the Western Isles?" *No idea Never been there laughs*

She looked serious. This was getting a bit worrying. I could see I was getting into a closed game. Another sandwich was required, I thought, to deflect from the path this seemed to be going. But as I extended my arm and opened my mouth to ask for another they both started and looked at my wrist and the one called Flory said,

"Sir what is that bracelet on your arm? It is highly unusual."

"It's just a quartz solar-powered watch. They're great, never needs batteries, just a bit of sunshine which I must say we seem to be getting our fair share of today".

--- ~ ---

E.

He was very relaxed in his manner and had the air of someone to whom I thought the world had been kind. His face was clean and closely shaven and his hair despite being unoiled was neat, tidy and well cut. His hands and nails had the marks of a gentleman. But as he rather impertinently outstretched his arm, for another sandwich, without asking first, I noticed a large bracelet clasping what looked like a jewelled blue disk. Flory asked him what it was, to which he replied with an incomprehensible phrase – I presumed he had forgotten himself and slipped back into his Scottish vernacular. I tried again.

"Please excuse me but what is it for?"

"Erm, well, to tell the time."

He looked at me puzzled as though it was the most obvious thing in the world.

I persisted.

"Pray forgive me, I didn't mean to enquire so closely but it is fascinating."

"Do you want to have a look? I must admit I don't normally get girls interested in my watches."

And then he unclasped it from his wrist and offered it to me. It had a peculiar flexible bracelet made of grey metal links clasping the small dark blue disc. I looked closer.

"Oh, it is a little clock!" I exclaimed.

"Pardon?"

He was quite taken aback. I looked again. I could see now it had tiny clock hands which glowed in the sunlight under a glass cover, but the time was incorrect.

"It is very beautiful, but how do you adjust the hands?"

"I don't. It's a radio-controlled watch. They move themselves. Haven't had to adjust it in over a year."

"But your bracelet, or watch as you call it, says a quarter past twelve, Mr Urquhart, while as you can see from the clubhouse clock it is now a quarter past two."

Puzzled, he removed a thin black case from his jacket pocket, looked at it then looked at the bracelet.

"Nope, it's right. I expect you will find that clubhouse clock has been stuck like that for years."

At this point my cousin Henry wandered over swinging his bat with a smile on his face. No doubt pleased that he'd whacked the ball into Granny Winshall's garden again.

"I hoped you enjoyed my game Elizabeth. I thought I'd better give the locals a bit of a chance otherwise they won't turn up next year."

"Of course, Henry. By the way this is James Urquhart. He was passing through, so we offered him a sandwich."

Henry stared at him.

"I'll be damned if he is!"

--- ~ ---

J.

I startled. He looked me closely in the eye.

"I'm sorry, I thought we were all making up names and titles as part of the afternoon fun".

The three of them looked at me in complete disbelief. Elizabeth said,

"Are you implying we are not who we say we are?"

"No, no," I protested feeling the hole I had dug getting deeper. "Oh, alright, I give up. My father was a draughtsman and my mother a telephonist. So, what are your real names?"

Elizabeth looked shocked. "Pardon? Are you suggesting we are also tradespeople, sir, masquerading as gentlefolk?"

Oh dear, I seemed to have stumbled into the Bullingdon club annual cricket bash. This was not the time for class action. I swallowed my pride.

"Look, I really apologise. I had no idea. I will leave immediately".

I touched my forelock with as much mockery as possible when facing a real hooray henry on his own ground with a cricket bat.

They all looked very confused. I rose to go.

Out of Time

---~---

E.

He looked quite frightened. I'd feared Henry was going to hit him with his bat or box his ears.

"Henry, stop! The man said he made a mistake. I think he genuinely thought he was at a village fete or carnival. You know, Henry, like at Lurgashall at St John's feast when all the parishioners dress up and ape their betters. Is that not right, Mr Urquhart?"

"Er, yes, that's right. Sorry, I don't come from these parts and I was lost".

Henry glowered at him but thankfully loosened his grip on the bat and, with a curt adieu and with a look of raised eyebrows at us, walked off to the club house.

"I apologise for my cousin. I do not know why your name caused such a reaction, though I must admit we are more than a little insulted to have our Sunday best compared with fancy dress."

He looked shaken.

"Look, Mr Urquhart, sit down again and have your lemonade. I think we have all made a mistake."

He hesitated, looked at his bracelet, looked at the club clock, puzzled and put it back on his wrist.

"OK thank you. Look, it was all a mistake on my part but I must be going soon otherwise my friends will be looking for me."

Then he inexplicably removed his jacket and sat down in just his vest!

"Mr Urquhart, your manners! Pray put on your jacket. You are not with your friends now!"

He was now looking very vexed and confused but nevertheless put his jacket back on.

But just as he sat down and I thought some semblance of normality was restored I heard what sounded like a bell coming from his jacket.

"Excuse me, I'd better take this. I expect it's my friends wondering where I am."

He reached inside and retrieved the black case he had looked at previously. He touched it and just as I was going to admonish him for taking out a cigarette and smoking in front of us he put it to his ear! Then a voice as if by magic inexplicably came from it.

"Oi! Jimbo! Where are you? We've been looking for you for over an hour."

He then looked at the case and spoke to it!

"You won't believe this Mike but I'm in the middle of a field with the Bullingdon Club eating cucumber sandwiches with two very nice young ladies."

"Yeah? Well while you are dancing around the maypole with your fairy friends we are in the Lammastide and it's your round."

"OK; see you in a bit once I've found out where I am."

Flory and I looked around us but saw no one else. Flory even looked under the table just in case a person was hiding there.

Without a word of apology or explanation for this interruption he turned the black case towards us and said, "Do you mind if I take a couple of photos of you otherwise they'll think I made this whole story up?"

Before I could say a word he held the case in front of us. It had a black shiny appearance like a dark mirror. Then he handed it to me.

"There - quite flattering really, mmh, you look a bit shocked. What do you think?"

What I was thinking I don't know. The black surface now

had a coloured picture of Flory and I with rather a stunned expression on our faces.

"You're right. Could do better. Give us a smile."

He then stood and proceeded to point the case at us from different angles which seemed so preposterous that we eventually broke into laughter.

"Pray stop, Mr Urquhart, you're acting too much the fool."

"OK, what do you think? The last couple look the best."

Once again he showed us the case but this time he ran his finger across it and with each stroke was a new picture of us, all from different angles.

"Well, sir, I have never seen such a contraption. What is it?"

"It's a Samsung S3."

Again he seemed to have slipped into his vernacular.

"I see. Well Mr Urquhart, we must leave you now as the sun is getting quite oppressive. We must prepare afternoon tea, and you will want to return to your friends."

"I'm not surprised wearing all those clothes in this heat. How many layers have you got on underneath?"

Flory and I looked at each other and she held my hand. I looked over to the club house to catch Henry's eye but he was engaged in conversation. I would have to defend our honour myself.

"Pardon me, Mr Urquhart, but we are not accustomed to this type of conversation. You have been over familiar, lied about your family, sat down improperly dressed and taken a sandwich without asking and then you enquire into our personal habits. Good day to you!"

But instead of going he just slumped down into the chair totally dejected.

---~---

J.

I gave up. This was a whole new madness. I said,

"Well, I can see I've totally over stepped the mark, ladies. Ok, goodbye then. Enjoy the cricket and, oh, thanks for the lemonade and sandwiches."

I then slowly walked over to the cart where the two old farm hands were still sitting. I asked where the Lammastide was and they pointed down the road.

"About half a mile, you can't miss it, still has most of its thatch on."

As I walked down the road, feeling a bit sorry for myself and angry at the girls, the cool breeze returned, wafting in my face, and an old MG whizzed past with what looked like another member of the Bolongers on his way to the fete. He gave me a wave. I reached for my phone to let my friends know I was coming, hoping there would still be time for a pint.

Damn! No phone!

Panic! I must have left it on the table. Oh god, do I go back for further stick or just buy a new phone. Obviously, it was stick. I reluctantly turned back leaving the thought of a cool pint behind me.

--- ~ ---

E.

"Well really, Flory that is the most peculiar man I have ever met."

"Yes but apart from his appalling manners he seemed to be quite harmless."

"Yet ... I must admit there was something refreshing about him or dare I say, agreeable. I felt it was an air of simple ignorance. Judging by his hands he looked well bred."

"Perhaps he has spent a long time abroad away from society.

It would account for the attention he gave you when he arrived at our table."

I pretended that I had not noticed.

"Or maybe it was just his Scottish manners."

"Now, we must join Henry now at the clubhouse and listen to his tales of prowess on the field."

"Yes, and we must not forget to listen with awe and fascination."

As I picked up my parasol I noticed something under the table.

"Flory! Look, it is Mr Urquhart's black case."

"Ooh, let's have a look at those pictures again, Elizabeth."

But there were no pictures, just a shiny black surface with what looked like a little clock still telling the wrong time.

"We must return it, Flory. Take it over to old Ted and tell him to take it to the Lammastide, ask for a James Urquhart and make all haste."

I fumbled in my purse. "Here's a shilling for his trouble. Go on, quick!"

---~---

J.

I eventually returned to the green. The old cart was still there by the roadside, but the farmers had gone. Even worse as I turned the corner of the copse I was greeted with an empty field. Everyone had gone! I hastened over to the club house. The clock still said 14:15. The wooden building was silent but I still tried the door. Locked. I turned around and scanned the grounds. Suddenly I noticed in the far corner of the green the MG again with the driver leaning against the door enjoying a fag. I walked quickly over to him.

"Hello old boy, can I help?" he said. "You look like you've lost your horse."

Oh dear, it seemed they were all out today. I decided to ignore it.

"Excuse me, but do you know where the people playing cricket here have gone?"

"Sorry, old chap. Just got here. Seen no one - except you, of course. Don't think there was a game here this Sunday, anyway. If there is a party they'll be all over at Lurgashall, I expect, for the shoot."

I seemed to be living on the wrong planet.

"Look, you couldn't do me a favour? I think I've left my phone with a girl who was here this afternoon."

"That's a good wheeze, old sport. Hoping she'd contact you, eh?"

"Yeah, except she can't ring me 'cos she's got my phone, hasn't she?" Hoping he would get the blindingly obvious.

"What? Oh yes. Look, borrow mine, give her a bell. If she's got it, she'll pick it up."

I accepted graciously and rang my phone. No answers so I recorded a message.

"Hi, this is James. Er, James Urquhart. If you are the lovely ladies who have found my phone could you give me a ring at home tonight on 012...... Oh, by the way, apologies if I was out of order and thanks for the sandwiches."

I rang off.

"Thanks very much, mate."

"No probs and good luck. Where's your car?"

I'd forgotten about my car.

"About two miles away at Petworth."

"You look like you need a lift. Hop in."

I was very grateful.

---~---

E.

The club house was full. ~~The schools had broken up~~ as ~~there were children everywhere~~ we on holiday. The villagers had been invited in and were enjoying the beer and afternoon tea.

Just then old Ted came through the door looking a little sheepish.

"Did you find him, Ted?"

"I'm sorry, my lady, but no one answered to that name nor had the customers heard of him."

"Oh well, ah, thank you Ted. You can keep the shilling for your troubles."

When we returned to the Lodge we went immediately up to Flory's room where we quickly took out the black case and placed it carefully on the dressing table. I touched the smooth, black mirror face gingerly and the little clock appeared again.

Suddenly it moved. We both jumped, and a tinkling sound came out of it, as we had heard that afternoon.

"Oh Elizabeth, what is it doing?"

"Shhh! I think it is going to speak again."

But after a few moments the bell stopped and then a tiny message appeared on the black mirror.

We tentatively looked closer to read what it said.

"Missed Call – ring Johnny."

Before I could stop her, Flory touched the message.

The screen changed and a green picture appeared accompanied by a purring sound.

"Flory, what have you done?"

Then a voice.

"Hi, Johnny here. Where are you, James? Have you found those lovely ladies who stole your phone?"

Lovely ladies? Stole? We looked at each other. I put my face close to the mirror and said, "Excuse me, sir, but I don't think we've met." I said.

"No, we haven't, but it sounds like I'd like to."

We felt we had had more than enough familiarity today.

"Sir, we have Mr. Urquhart's black case. Kindly tell us how we can return it."

"What? Oh yes, well just ring James on 012— —— and tell him you've got his phone. I'm sure he'll be grateful."

"Excuse me sir, but we don't know what you mean. What is a phone?"

"What?? The thing you are speaking to. Are you for real? How old are you?"

"Sir, I assure we are quite real and I take great exception to someone asking our age! Are all Mr. Urquhart's friends so rude?"

Silence. Then it spoke again.

"Look, sorry, I'm just the messenger. Now, let me think. You really don't know how to use a phone?"

"No sir, I told you."

"OK, looks like I'm going to really need to squeeze the old lemon for this one. Right, get a pen and paper and write this down. You can write, can't you?"

Flory just stopped my grabbing the case and throwing it at the wall. I went to the desk and selected a good pen and paper.

"I'm ready, sir."

He then gave a series of strange instructions to use on the black case. Press this, press that, press these numbers, etc.

"And don't forget," he said, "If the screen goes blank, wipe your finger across the screen to get it back."

"Thank you, sir. But if we get it wrong what shall we do?"

"Good point. I'll ring you back in half an hour to check. Good luck."

"Oh, just a minute, the mirror is black!"

"Don't worry, just wipe your finger across it and it will come back. Got it? Good. Bye."

We sat down and began to follow the instructions.

A picture of Mr Urquhart appeared on the screen with a long number. He was displayed with a large red pointed hat on his head. He was holding a tankard in one hand and the other had his thumb pointing up. He seemed very happy. I pressed the green button and after a moment I heard the buzzing sound again.

---∼---

J.

I had just gotten in when the land line rang.

"Hi, Jim here."

"Is that Mr Urquhart?"

"Yes."

"It is Miss Bicester, Elizabeth Bicester, here Mr Urquhart. I have your black case."

"My what?"

"You know, the thing I'm speaking to you on."

"Oh great, you found my phone. I came back but you had all gone. Must have been a good party at the shoot."

"I did not go to a shoot as you say, but it was an interesting afternoon."

"For me, too. So how can I pick up my phone?"

"You could come to the lodge. I'll give it to one of the servants."

"Sorry, I didn't realise I had annoyed you so much."

"What do you mean?"

"You could give it to me in person."

There was a brief silence followed by a faint whispering which sounded like an argument, then she spoke again.

"Will you be on your own?"

"Yes, though I can bring a friend for your sister Flory, if you like?"

"Certainly not, Mr Urquhart! I will meet you at the tradesman's entrance. And I will be with one of the servants."

"OK. By the way where is this lodge?"

"Why, it's the Lodge at Hamgreen".

"Hamgreen? No probs, I'm only in Chichester. I'll be there in half an hour."

"But Mr Urquhart, that's over ten miles!"

"Don't worry, the roads are good at this time of the day. See you then. Bye".

---~---

E.

I looked at Flory.

"He said he will be here in half an hour. I don't know how but we should prepare; he may only be pretending he's in Chichester".

I touched the black glass again.

"Look, there is a list of people with pictures of themselves, Flory".

He seemed to know a lot of ladies, though I must admit I did not approve of the state of their dress.

I accidentally pressed one. The phone began to buzz again. A lady's voice spoke.

"Hi, Jim, what you phoning me now for? I'm in traffic on the M4."

I could hear music and a strange roaring sound. Before I could reply the lady spoke again.

"Jim! Jim? God, the idiot's sat on his phone again."

And then it was silent.

---~---

J.

It was an easy drive up to the lodge. I turned on to the gravel drive and cut the engine. It looked empty save for a light in one of the ground-floor rooms. It was quite an old place, Georgian probably. Grade 2 at least with ashlar walls.

I went around the side and found what looked like the tradesmen's door and pressed the bell. After a while the door opened and an old chap appeared wearing what looked like the clothes of the asset-rich and cash-poor. His hair had receded someway on his head and to compensate he had grown a rather an unkempt forked beard and straggly whiskers to match. For some reason he looked familiar.

"Hi, I was told to come around here, is this the tradesman's entrance?"

"Pardon?"

"Sorry, I was told by the lady who lives here to meet her here. She has my phone you see."

I could see that he didn't see.

"Sorry, I'll start again. I lost my phone and a girl called Elizabeth Bicester found it and told me to come here to collect it."

"There is no Bicester here". He had that rather clipped Edinburgh accent you hear from Scots who have been exposed to too much to the English.

This day was going crazy.

"Look, I might have the wrong address. Is this Hamgreen Lodge?"

"Yes, but I can assure you there are no women here."

"OK. Would you mind if I use your phone so I can clean up this mess?"

He looked at me suspiciously, trying to decide whether I was out to rob his house. Then said, "Follow me."

I followed the old chap into a small hallway. It had the air of one of those faded country mansions which hadn't had the fortune to be done up by the National Trust. The walls or wall paper were that faded green you see in every Georgian house and beside the inner door, a table and cabinet that looked like they were from the same period but had suffered too many house moves.

I picked up the phone and dialled my number.

It picked up and I heard Elizabeth's voice.

"Elizabeth? Sorry, I seem to have come to the wrong house."

"Where are you?"

"Hamgreen Lodge."

"But that's where I am too."

We were both silent for a moment, trying to work out who had it wrong

"Elizabeth, are you still there?"

"Yes, I am by the pantry door, but I cannot see you."

"I must be at the wrong entrance. Describe it to me, you know the whole room."

"Er, green walls, a glass cabinet and a small dresser."

I looked around me; it was exactly as she described it.

Then I noticed the old chap had been listening in. For some reason he was looking as worried as me.

If I was being set up then this was getting to be an expensive joke.

I rang off, apologised for disturbing him and drove off home. No one's going to believe this, I thought. Better get the phone blocked.

---~---

Out of Time

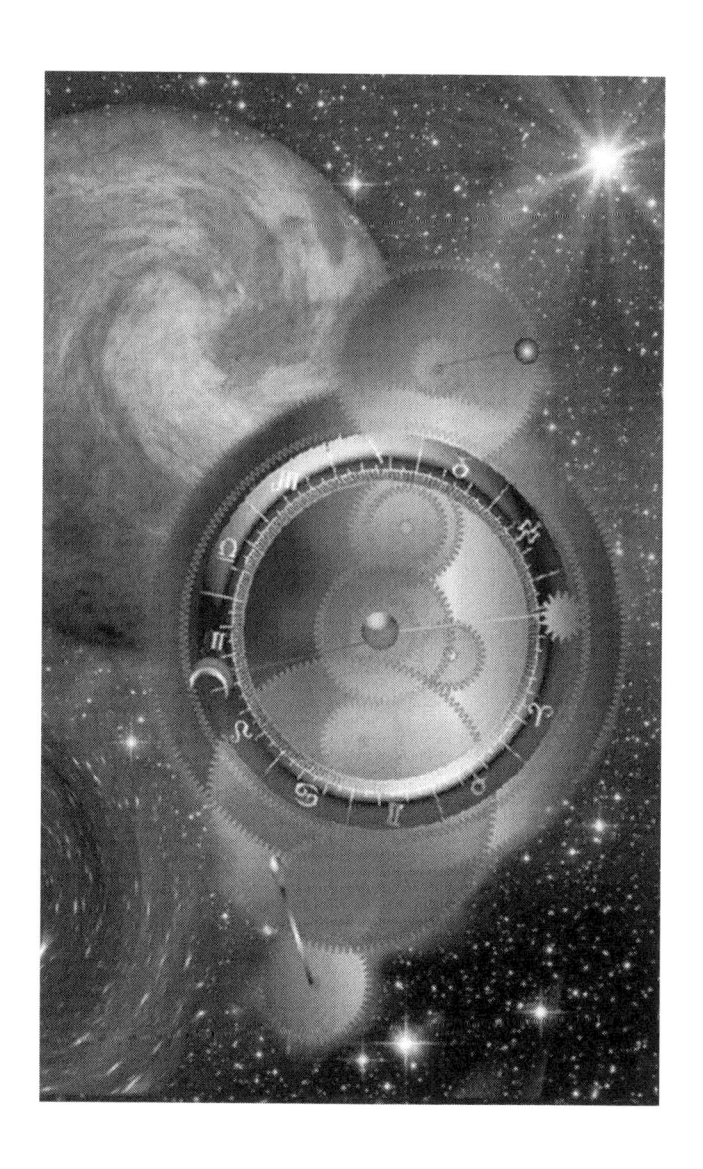

Out of Time

Chapter Two

E.

His voice had disappeared. We looked at each other. –"He must be around the back of the lodge, Flory!"

We searched the ground floor rooms, looking out of the windows, then went into the garden. No one.

I was at a loss. Was this some strange game? If it was, I could not understand it.

"Try contacting him again, Elizabeth."

I tried again but there was no answer.

I sat down nonplussed then Flory said she had an idea.

"If you really want to return this case we can try the railway station at Chichester tomorrow. Remember he did say he was travelling from Chichester but also that he was not from around here. He may have arrived by train recently."

"Yes, they may recognise him and know where he is staying."

The next morning Smethers drove us into the market town. Unfortunately, our enquiries at the railway station did not lead to success and so reluctantly at noon we rendezvoused with some of our friends for a picnic luncheon in the Priory Park. We spent much time recounting our adventures which were received with interest though not necessarily with much credulity.

"And you say this black case allows one to speak to someone at a distance?" said Albert, who I had noticed recently had been showing interest towards Flory.

"Only certain people," I replied.

"Then let us try to contact him now," he said.

"I do not have it with me. It is at the lodge for safe keeping.

I have tried twice but to no avail."

"Is this one of your silly practical jokes, Elizabeth?"

"No, it is not! It is all true, isn't it, Flory?"

I could see they were beginning to doubt our story but just then I thought I spied him again. He was wearing different clothes. I was glad to see him a little smarter than yesterday and he was conversing with a strangely dressed young gentleman. When I thought he had turned in my direction I waved.

---~---

J.

When I got home it was quite late and my sister Jill was curled up on the sofa eating Hobnobs.

"Had a good evening?" I said.

"You don't want to know. How about you? You haven't been out frightening the young ladies of Chi again?"

"Funny you should mention that but ..."

"God, is that the time? Time for bed for me. Don't forget we are seeing the estate agent in the morning."

"Damn I forgot."

The next morning we drove down to Chichester and after seeing the estate agent picked up some sandwiches from Subway and strolled into the park off North Street.

And there were the two girls again sitting with a group all dressed in similar clothes to those I had seen them in at the cricket club.

"Jill, see that group over there?"

"What, the pretentious ones dressed up like it's the Goodwood Revival?"

"Yeah, they must all be down here for some special toffs' event. I met them up at Hamgreen during our ramble yesterday."

"You must have looked a bit odd in your hiking gear."

"Yeah – tell me about it! Anyway, see the one on the left in the powder blue dress? I think she has my phone."

"Must have been some party. I thought your phone was surgically attached to your body. Anyway, only one way to find out. Let me ring your phone."

Just then Elizabeth waved at me.

"Looks like your new girlfriend has seen you. Let's go over and say hello. I like to see who can get your phone off you."

"Ok, let's find out what they are playing at. Word of warning though. They act posh and are very prudish."

"Sure you just didn't just overstep the mark with your banter?"

"Come to think of it, I did ask them what they were wearing underneath all that finery."

"Still as smooth as ever, eh Jim? Far be it from me to give you advice on your predatory habits but I suggest dropping 'Are you wearing knickers?' as your opening gambit."

--- ~ ---

E.

He waved back at us, then he and the young gentleman with him walked over to us. As they drew nearer I suddenly realised that his friend was actually a young woman. Her short hair and her trousers had confused me. In fact, on closer inspection I realised she was wearing thick black stockings under a very short skirt or kilt and a black vest, which to my embarrassment was cut to reveal her shoulders and significant portion of her neck and bust!

"Hello Elizabeth, hello Flory." He said. "Still in fancy dress I see. Another charity do I suppose."

He saw my perplexed look and checked himself.

"Oh I forgot, where are my manners. This is my sister, Jill."

I nodded trying not look at her body and wondering why he had allowed his sister, (if she was!) to wear such a provocative outfit in public. Was his sister one of those "actresses" I had read about? I had never seen a woman dressed so scantily in public and was bemused that he allowed her to accompany him without any sign of embarrassment.

But before I could say anything his sister began to speak in the same familiar manner as James.

"Yep, I'm his sister. Purveyor of all my girl friends who end up battered on his rocky shore. She gave him a mildly accusing look, and then continued. "So, I hear you may have James' phone. Good move, usually his girlfriends only manage to get his phone number. His text history would be worth a fortune to some I know."

This language was beyond me. I looked at Flory for support but she was equally nonplussed.

"I'm afraid I do not quite follow. Yes, I do have Mr Urquhart's black case which I believe is called a "phone" but I have left it for safe keeping at the Lodge."

"So how do we get it back?" he said with a worried look. "I've already been there once, and you weren't there!"

"So you say, Mr Urquhart, but I can assure we were there and you did not turn up!"

He turned to his sister for help, who gave a look that suggested she did not wholly believe his story either. Then he tried again. "Maybe I can drive you back to the Lodge so we don't lose each other again."

"Sir, you do not think that I would go gallivanting off with a stranger unaccompanied, do you?!"

"My sister does it all the time!"

His sister gave him a look which I can only describe as amusement rather than the shock such a slur on her character should have produced.

"Look, if you are concerned about my intentions ... "

At this point his sister shook her head and rolled her eyes up at me as if to apologise for him and said, "Look, please excuse my brother, how about if I come with you?"

"Yeah, I'll bring my sister Jill. I have it on good authority she is quite safe with other women and you can bring your sister Flory. Then I will be safely outnumbered three to one."

I listened to this offer with some trepidation, but I could see that they were as genuinely perplexed by the situation as we were. Flory and I looked at each other.

"I suppose we could, though we insist that Smethers follows us in his carriage."

They both looked around and looked quite surprised to see our carriage by the edge of the park where Smethers was feeding the horses.

"What, that contraption there?" he said. "I hope he can keep up."

Then he reverted to his manners of yesterday.

"Do you wish to change first into your normal clothes or are you going back like that?"

"Mr Urquhart that is the third time you have referred to our clothes. I can only think that it may be normal where you come from, but it is not so in Sussex."

"I was only worried about you getting into my car."

His sister intervened again. "I do apologise for my brother. All he wants is his phone back. Without it his whole social life, as he calls it, will collapse."

"Very well," I said. "We will accompany you. If only so we can resolve this problem once and for all!"

We walked over to our carriage and I told Smethers we were going in Mr Urquhart's carriage and he was to follow us closely.

We then accompanied Mr Urquhart and his sister into the Wynd which lead to North Street, but when we turned into a large courtyard there were stationed in rows, to our intense surprise, the most unusual carriages, or dare I say contraptions, I have ever seen! Each carriage looked like a gigantic ostrich egg with a long bulbous nose punctuated by sealed dark windows. Most of them were very small, certainly less than head height, and the undercarriage no more than a foot above the ground supported near each corner with tiny wheels made of a thick black patterned material. They did not seem suitable for travel save in a town with well-made cobbled roads. The surfaces of the carriages were varnished in a variety of colours and were so well polished that they reflected their surrounds. On the front and back two or four lamps enclosed the body with no obvious means of lighting the candles. But what was most baffling was that there were no attachments for the horses. Nor did I see any drivers or porters!

Before I could say anything he produced what looked like a key and when he pressed it, orange lights lit up at the corners of one of the carriages. He motioned us towards it. "Here's our car. Front or back, ladies?"

I was completely confused but before I could say anything he stepped forward and opened a door, inviting us to enter the carriage. Inside were snug black leather contoured seats. We were rather hesitant at first as there seemed to be very little room but his sister allayed our fears by opening the front door and, ducking down, slid into the seat. I realised now their clothes were obviously fashioned for travelling in such vehicles.

"I suggest, ladies that you take your hats off before getting in as there may not be enough room for them."

We could see looking inside that there was no option but to comply and with a mild look of disapproval and resignation we withdrew our hat pins and removed our hats.

Then rather than having the manners to look away, he stared at our hair with what I can only say was an extremely approving look even though I could feel one or two of my ringlets had fallen on to my face.

We eventually managed to arrange ourselves in the seats by spreading our skirts in a rather unglamorous arrangement. James sat in the front. I was glad he did not regard our discomfort.

There was then much confusion as he insisted that we fit ourselves into some sort of harness. We declined his offer to help rather vigorously and were relieved when his sister came to our rescue.

Then he pressed a button and the roar of an engine could be heard, and to our complete surprise the carriage inexplicably began to move forward. I could see James was guiding it by means of the wheel in front of him though I could not see the means of propulsion. All I could think of was that it was propelled by some kind of new-fangled steam engine. We moved very quickly until to my surprise we came to a road where literally dozens of these horseless carriages drove past at incredible speeds. There were also people everywhere dressed like James and his sister.

"Where are we, Mr Urquhart? This looks like Chichester, but it has changed completely."

"Don't tell the locals – they've been fighting to keep it the same for the last hundred years!"

Suddenly he turned the carriage on to a great highway and accelerated up to an impossibly high speed.

"If the roads are ok we should be Hamgreen in about half an hour," he said.

The trees and houses sped past us like a blur. Yet there was hardly any feeling of speed or wind. James seemed very relaxed as though he was just sitting in an armchair looking out of a window. Now and again another carriage came towards us. Each time I had to close my eyes. It passed us impossibly close.

"Mr Urquhart, what speed are we travelling?"

"Oh, about fifty miles an hour."

"You mean we could travel fifty miles in one hour!"

"Yeah, do you want go faster?"

"Certainly not, Mr Urquhart. This is quite dangerous enough!"

"OK then. Would you like me to play some music?"

"Pardon?"

"You know - what type, jazz, pop, classical?"

"Why, er, I think I prefer a romantic music. Why do you ask?" For I could not see any musical instruments in the cabin.

"How about Chopin?"

"Oh yes, I can play a little Chopin".

"Can you? Then you're the girl for me. You can come around any night and play Chopin. Mind, you will have to bring your own piano."

"Mr Urquhart, I am sure you mean well in your own fashion, but I think sometimes you speak a little too plainly for your own good."

Jill nudged him in the ribs. "That's telling you, Jim."

"Point taken, Miss Bicester. Anyway, let's have look at what we've got."

And he pressed some buttons on a little window.

"Ah! Here's some Chopin piano."

And suddenly I was immersed in the sound of a pianist playing a Chopin nocturne. The aural sensation was so strong my eyes closed instantly and I felt myself fall through space and transported to a wood-panelled music room with tall French windows where Chopin himself was sitting at a grand piano playing just for me. As I fell deeper in my revelry, dappled sun beams pierced the garden windows and began to dance on the timbered floor. And as I watched them mesmerised, I sensed a fragrance of honeysuckle drifting in from a garden whose leaves caressed the window panes, beckoning me. Oh what joy! I could have stayed there for ever.

Then all too soon we were at Hamgreen!

The music instantly stopped, and I woke from my revelry. "Mr Urquhart that is the most beautiful music I have ever heard."

"Oh thanks," he said, in a tone as though it was commonplace to provide such magical effects. "I've plenty more. Anyway, now you need to guide me along to the Lodge. We need to make sure we get it right this time."

I showed him the way until we turned into the Lodge drive.

"Is this the lodge, Elizabeth?"

"Yes it is, though it seems for some reason a little untidy. It must be the afternoon light."

"Well, we'd better go in."

---~---

J.

I parked the car at some distance from the Lodge and once we'd disentangled the ladies from the safety belts, which you would have thought they'd never seen before, we began to walk up the drive.

Jill said to me, "Your music selection certainly has improved. There may be hope for you yet. They seem to be quite affected. Much better than the time we took our cousin Annabelle to that party when you 'inadvertently' played the Bloodhound Gang's Discovery Channel."

"Oh god! I remember. It was her 18th birthday. Put the

wrong CD in. Couldn't turn it off. Did she not end up in a Nunnery?"

"No she did not, Jim, but no thanks to you."

Suddenly the front door opened and the man I had seen the previous night appeared.

"Hello again, what do you want this time?"

I turned to Elizabeth expectantly, but to my consternation she seemed rather frightened.

"Excuse me, Sir," she said, "but I live here."

"Excuse me but I don't think you do and I would appreciate it if you got off my land before I call the police!"

"OK mate," I said, "Looks like we've made a mistake but this lady says she left my phone here."

"I very much doubt it, I've been here all week."

We looked at each other and Jill whispered, "I don't know about you, Jim, but I think we've got a couple of nutters here. I think we'd better get back to the car."

I turned to Elizabeth and Flory.

"But this is our house, Mr Urquhart. We have lived here all our lives!"

"Well, I think we should leave and go and think what to do. He's beginning to look a bit angry."

"Are you not going to defend us, Mr Urquhart?"

"What, start a fight?"

"Yes, and show him the door."

"I'm afraid I'm not into fisticuffs without a good reason. I prefer to use my running legs."

"Do you not believe us?"

"Yes, but maybe we should go and find out why he is here and not letting you in his house. Now please get in the car."

"Well really! Miss Urquhart, you must be ashamed of him!"

"Only when he's trying it on with my girlfriends."

I took Elizabeth's arm. Her eyes were vacant and a look of

shock was on her face. There was something plainly wrong here that needed explanation.

"Come on, Elizabeth, let's go and work out a plan of action. There's nothing we can do here."

---∼---

E.

He gently guided me back to the carriage. I didn't resist. Flory was crying. We drove more slowly back to Chichester and in silence. The road was surprisingly empty of traffic, which allowed me to gaze out of the window and contemplate the extraordinary events at our home. There was something wrong with my world. Everything was out of joint. Even the countryside had changed. Enormous fields with uniform regimented crops stretched over the Downs as far as the eye could see, which despite our speed seemed to appear and drift past in slow motion, yet I saw no one working in them. Where were the little fields and flowering mists of poppies and cornflowers? The absence of traffic and people accompanied by the smoothness of the road and the emptiness of the landscape made me begin to suspect I was trapped in some phantasmagorical dream and that when I awoke I would find myself in my own bed at Hamgreen. Except I was not want to wake up. Then as we came into Chichester the spell was broken by a lady crossing the road which made James break and speak quite violently for which he quickly apologised.

We arrived at his house, which was actually one of a row of small cottages. I expected a larger house for such an unusual carriage. The rooms were rather small, though cosy and lined with books. He apologised for the untidiness which I had not noticed and asked us to make ourselves comfortable. It reminded me of Uncle William's study in Bicester, except here and there were miniatures of Pre-Raphaelite paintings which

I could only presume were expensive reproductions, and the wallpaper was very avant-garde, consisting of intertwined leaves and trellis work which I had seen in London, and demonstrated that despite their unusual manners they were well versed in the latest fashion. His sister, who had shown much concern for our plight on the way back, was good enough to ask us if would like to change out of our clothes and perhaps wash.

"You must be boiled in all that gear," she said.

They both seemed to have quite an unhealthy interest in our clothing. Nevertheless, I felt that we needed to change into something more suitable for the late afternoon.

"I agree we are quite warm from these exertions but we only have these clothes since we cannot get into our house. We do not even have garments to receive let alone any clothes for the evening!"

"Don't worry", said his sister, "you can borrow some of mine. Looking at you they should easily fit."

We thanked her doubtfully, not at all sure that the clothes she might possess would be at all suitable for us

"Oh, but excuse me, Miss Urquhart," I said, "but where are your maids? Do you not have a maid to help you dress?"

Mr Urquhart apologised and said with a smile that he had been trying to get a maid in for some time but his sister refused to have one in the cottage.

I looked hesitantly at his sister. "You mean we must dress ourselves?"

"Don't worry. I'll help."

I looked at him. Her sister saw my look.

"Oh, don't worry about Jim. He's well trained. If he knows my girlfriends are running about in a state of undress he will stay downstairs out of the way like a pet dog. Isn't that right, Jim?"

"Absolutely! Never a peek except when Jill's not looking".

I was beginning to understand that much of their conversation was, although at times rather burlesque, only meant in humour. Wherever they originated from, it seemed that ladies and gentlemen talked to each other as though they were talking to their own kind. In some ways this seemed to make it much easier to talk between the sexes. Though I reminded myself that I must be careful if I joined in such a conversation for I should not want to compromise my honour in public.

We went upstairs with Jill and started to try to undress, which was quite difficult without a maid.

"Here", said Jill, "Let me help. My god, is that a real bustle? And how many petticoats are you wearing? And is that a real laced bodice?"

"Yes, Miss Urquhart, and that is why we need a maid to undo it."

"Don't worry, let me have a go. There you go. Gosh! You don't believe in shaving, do you?"

"Pardon?"

"And what is that perfume? It smells of lavender and carbolic soap!"

We were very much taken aback as we had spent some time preparing ourselves for the day's outing and I had been assured by the Ladies Magazine that my friend Clara had brought from London that sandalwood and lavender was the fashion in eau de cologne.

"I hope you don't mind but I think what both of you need is a good shower. Come on into the bathroom. Jim!"

"Yes Jill, want some help?"

"No. Nudie girl alert. Keep your wandering eyes averted!"

"You can trust me," I heard him shout back.

We had never seen so many bottles of lotions, perfumes and

soaps.

"Those two bottles in the corner are Jim's'. I replenish them each birthday and Christmas. All the rest are for us. Just help yourselves."

"I am sorry, Ms Urquhart, but where do we start? There is so much from which to choose!"

"Well first have a shower."

At one end of the room was a glass partition. Ms Urquhart slid a door to its side to reveal a tiled cubicle with what I quickly recognised was a canopy shower similar to those recently introduced into the better suites of hotels in the West End. I was a little nervous at first as my brief experience of one had been blessed with only two flows, deluge or off. The deluge option, I swear, had a malevolent mind of its own, imparting at irregular intervals scalding hot or freezing water which if one was not prepared necessitated a quick exit accompanied by exclamations which until then I had not thought I was capable of speaking. I can only presume the inventor had got the idea from observing the washing of sheep at a country market. However, when Jill showed me its operation I indulged in it with pleasure, I could see why such a thing if designed properly could become popular.

I was a little concerned by how much hot water I should use but Ms Urquhart generously said that we could use as much as we liked until the water in the Sussex Downs was exhausted. I must admit by the time we had finished I began to believe her. It must have been powered by a very large gas boiler and reservoir but where it was kept I could not ascertain.

With regards to the oils and lotions I think she almost gave us a look of despair but quickly checked herself and proceeded to describe what things were and in which order they should be used. It quickly became a game for Flory and I and we were soon enjoying refreshing ourselves. We could not believe the number of oils, solutions and aromas were available, though throughout our ablutions I must admit I kept a nervous eye on the door.

---~---

J.

They must have been up there for almost two hours. Eventually Jill came down.

"God, what a pair! I genuinely think they've never dressed themselves in their lives, let alone washed properly. I am certain that their clothes smelt of mothballs. It reminded me of old gran's wardrobe. And you don't want to know the problems I had with the bras."

"You should have asked for help. I'm an expert in that area."

"Mmh not what I've heard, but I'm talking about putting them on. They looked like they'd never seen one before."

"Shh! I think they have finished at last."

"Keep a straight face, Jim. I think they are genuinely having a hard time."

Just then the door opened on the landing and Elizabeth called if it was alright to come down.

They both came down slowly together, rather nervously I thought. They had managed to put on a couple of Jill's long-sleeved blouses which they had done up to the neck, and the longest skirts they could find which just managed to cover their knees, under which they were wearing a thick pair of Jill's winter stockings.

"They don't believe in revealing themselves, do they?"

"Shut up. They wouldn't wear anything shorter."

---~---

E.

Miss Urquhart's clothes were very comfortable and mysteriously stretched and contracted as we moved, though more material would have been welcome. The absence of over gowns was especially disconcerting, though Ms Urquhart eventually persuaded us that what we described as 'under clothing' was in fact normal wear for public display. I must admit like all ladies we like to emphasise our feminine attributes, but we felt that this fashion would leave too little for the imagination. Flory had tried some make up and failed and I told her to wash it off as, the painted face that Jill wore, was not for the likes of us. Ms Urquhart agreed, saying that gentleman preferred ladies to look natural, though it often took over an hour of preparation to achieve such an effect. We went down the stairs. I noticed he had stationed himself at what I thought was too advantageous a position in the hall, and I held my skirt as close as possible to my knees. I think he gave me a sympathetic look and was good enough to concentrate on my face.

"Mr Urquhart, I apologise for our appearance. Your sister was very kind and did the best she could with what she was admits is her meagre wardrobe."

"Meagre! What? Jill'? Promise me you won't show her your wardrobe."

"So Mr Urquhart ..."

"Please call me James or Jim. You're making me sound like an old school master."

"Well, if you insist. James, what are we to do? We are locked out of our house and our father will be distraught."

"And yet," he said, "we have been there and there was no Squire."

"It is beyond comprehension!"

"Not quite."

"What do you mean, James?"

"Do you notice it is getting dark?"

I looked around me. The sun was setting and an evening mist was rising.

"Yes, we should light the candles." I said, "I presume with no maid we must light them ourselves. But where are they?"

"There aren't any, Elizabeth."

"But ..."

"Watch."

And then he walked over to the door and pressed a button and lamps immediately lit around the room – "Oh, they are wonderful. How are they lit so quickly?"

"They are electric lights"

When he saw that I looked puzzled again he said softly, "Elizabeth, what year is it?"

"Why, 1873."

He held my gaze. He looked so sad.

"No, Elizabeth. Here it is the year 2015."

--- ~ ---

Out of Time

Chapter Three

E.

I looked around me. The horseless carriages, their clothes, their manner, the invisible music. I suddenly thought of that ghost of Dickens who transported Mr Scrooge to the future. Were these people phantoms come to take us out of our time?

I panicked and looked at Flory in the hope it was just me. But she was in the same shocked state.

"You have kidnapped us, Mr Urquhart! You have stolen us from our time, our world. Who are you all? Are you wraiths?"

He grabbed my hand.

"What, you think we are ghosts? What is to say you are not fairies or phantoms – and anyway, who stole me when I met you at the cricket?"

"We did not!" I protested. "We saw you. You were asking for us and you came straight to us. Oh, I wish Henry was here, Flory."

I tried to pull my hand away but he would not let go.

"Please believe me, Elizabeth," he said, in what I could see was some earnest. "I wouldn't kidnap you and would willingly take you back if I could."

I looked into his eyes. He looked almost as scared as I was.

"Elizabeth, may I call you Liz?"

"You most certainly cannot, Mr Urquhart! And please let go of my hand. Your familiarity is becoming exceedingly trying again."

"OK, sorry. Look, I promise I will do all I can to get you back."

I looked at his sister. She was as shocked as we and was staring at her brother with her mouth open.

"What did you just say, Jim?"

"I said," with a pause, "they are from different times, Jill. Somehow our times have overlapped."

His sister sat down. "I need a drink, Jim."

"Don't we all!"

He went to a cupboard and produced a bottle of wine and one of brandy.

"Both?" He said to his sister.

"Yes please Jim, and in a large glass."

An hour later the bottle of wine was empty and there was not much left in the brandy. Flory and I had taken a glass of wine each, but James and his sister looked like they could match my cousin Henry and his friends at one of their silly parlour drinking games.

"So," said James after much agitated discussion and holding his half-empty glass at a dangerous angle, "I have an exceedingly good idea."

"And what can that be, Mr Urquhart? Another abduction perhaps?"

He ignored my jibe.

"Where are you supposed to be tomorrow, ladies?"

"We were supposed to be meeting our cousin Henry for lunch after the shoot at Fittleworth."

"Then we will go there and meet them."

"But how? If what you say is true, we are in a different time by over a hundred years! Remember, when we went to the lodge it was not my time. Why do you think we will have success at Fittleworth?"

"Because I think we need to be at a place you would be expected to be before we met. And also, maybe it will also need to have some of the people who were at the cricket club. Were any of them with you at the picnic in Chichester, Elizabeth?"

"Why yes, James."

"Then we may be in luck. Shall we will try Fittleworth tomorrow?"

I looked at Flory then at Jill, who both shrugged their shoulders.

"I don't know, but it must be better than doing nothing."

The next morning was bright with a spring sunrise. I agreed with James that we should wear our proper clothes, for it would be very inappropriate to be found in his sister's attire with our friends. Though I must admit as we changed back into our own clothes they did not seem to feel as comfortable as they had been.

Jill tried to make us have another dowsing but we told her we were quite clean enough, thank you, and any more washing would completely remove our natural bodily oils.

While preparing ourselves for the day I noticed a photograph of Miss Urquhart with a gentleman on the landing. They seemed to be in the middle of a rather muddy field, scantily dressed and surrounded by hundreds of similarly dressed people. I hoped it was not one of those bacchanalia parties I had heard about in the bohemian outskirts of Middlesex. Jill noticed me regarding the photograph.

"That's my boyfriend, Liam, Elizabeth. Hard to imagine he's a policeman. It was the Osterley Jazz Festival. Rained all weekend. We got absolutely soaked."

I made a note to find out what jazz was as I felt that the dress code was a little beyond what I was prepared to wear. I took the opportunity to ask Jill about her courting and plans for the future.

"Oh yes, we've been going out for over two years. In fact, we are buying a house and hope to move in together this summer."

"And you are to be married soon?"

"Oh no, not yet," and then she looked at me and noticed my attention. "Oh I'm sorry, our society is possibly much more laissez-faire than yours."

"Please do not mistake our manners for prudishness. We know many couples who, as you put it, live together and quite openly. We may seem to be rather formal in our manners but they are very useful, for example for ascertaining whether a gentleman has humour, intelligence and of course wealth to support a family. I am sure that even now you have your own devices which achieve the same results."

"You know, you are quite right Elizabeth. You're very observant. And then of course, love comes along and ruins all our plans."

"Ha! Ha! How very true, Miss Urquhart."

"And how would you see Jim fitting into your plans?"

I suddenly felt the closeness of her look.

"Why, I hardly know him, Miss Urquhart."

We arrived at Fittleworth about one o'clock, in time for lunch. James parked his carriage by the old church and then we walked back down the byway to the coaching inn. As we arrived we could see, thank God, what looked like our party gathering. James and his sister held back for fear of drawing unwanted attention to their clothes.

Henry was standing by the porch with one of his shooting friends, Alfred, trying a pipe and when he saw us he waved and came running over to greet us.

"Elizabeth! Flory! Where have you been?"

We told him quickly that we had met an old aunt in Chichester and decided to stay overnight.

Then he spied James and his sister.

"And who are they?"

I told them they were my aunt's chauffeur and his sister who were on their way to market at Petworth for my aunt.

Henry looked rather coldly at James.

"So today you are a chauffeur, Mr Urquhart?"

James managed to hold his gaze and luckily held up my rather weak story. I distracted Henry from further interrogation by admonishing him about the evil smelling weed he was burning in his new pipe. Henry had recently taking up the habit and liked to think he was rather a connoisseur of pipes and the new American tobaccos. I knew that any questioning of this foul hobby immediately concentrated his mind on its defence at the expense of all other subjects.

---~---

J.

I listened to this conversation with some amusement.

Jill whispered, "Gosh, she can certainly think quickly on her feet, Jim. That was the quickest excuse I've ever heard for a dirty night stop-out. Watch out, Henry is coming towards us."

"Here's half a crown for your troubles, Mr Urquhart, and buy a hat and shirt and also a modest shawl for your sister," he said.

I had to grip Jill's arm quite tightly.

"Thank yee," I said and touched my forelock.

Elizabeth whispered, "James, you had better be off and thank you for your help, it was really appreciated."

"No problem Elizabeth, I mean Ms Bicester, and I hope we meet again."

And with that we went back to the car hidden behind the church. As I reached the road I said to Jill, "Let's wait here and see what happens."

But as I turned and looked back, to my horror they were

already gone! The time shift had collapsed. The pub was deserted save for a couple of cars parked at the front!

"My god, is that how it happens. That's unbelievable!"

"Well she's gone," I said. "We should have got her equivalent of a Filofax off her so we could find likely rendezvous points again."

"There's a chance she still has your phone."

"God yes! Well remembered. But only as long as the battery lasts."

We decided to try to phone her that evening. Twice there was no reply, then about 10 o'clock Elizabeth answered.

"James? Oh, I thought we had lost you."

"Quickly, Elizabeth, can you give me a list of times and dates where you will be meeting people from the cricket club?"

She paused and then gave a list of ten parties for the next month.

"Excellent," I said. "We'll try to meet up again. And I'll bring a new battery for your phone because it won't last much longer."

The arrangement was a success. We met Elizabeth several times after that, always making sure we left her with a freshly charged phone battery. On some occasions we dressed up in period costumes though our first attempt to blend in was nearly a disaster as our fashion, we quickly discovered, was at least ten years out of date. Jill thought I looked like Bertie Wooster's butler and Elizabeth thought Jill's fashion would have blended in with her mother's whist drive friends, but I thought it best not to pass that on.

On one occasion she took us to a small dinner party in Amberley. We had never been in a coach and horses before and I promised myself I would never complain about potholes again. The carriage followed the ruts rather than the road and I think it was only the spring-leaf suspension which stopped my teeth shaking out. Coupled with the thought that it was now dark and the road seemed to be lit by just two candle lamps to guide four horses hell-bent on getting to Amberley as fast as possible, I began to have some sympathy for Elizabeth's first ride in my car. Elizabeth noticed.

"You look a little ill James. I hope we are not going too fast for you."

There was no point in defending myself. "Apart from it's pitch black, I can't see anything out the windows, every creak and bump sounds like a wheel coming off and I believe the River Arun is on one side and a rife on the other waiting to swallow us up, I feel quite fine."

Jill, who up to this point had been rather silent and possibly regretting her decision to try out a whalebone corset, helped me out by saying, "And don't forget the phantom coach coming towards us in the opposite direction, Jim."

Elizabeth, who I could see was enjoying this, said. "So, James, travelling at only ten miles an hour gives you some trepidation but you are quite happy to travel at over fifty miles an hour without any qualms or concern for the safety of your passengers?"

I was about to talk about the improvements in road safety, air bags etc., but then remembered that over 300,000 had been killed and millions injured since the Second World War. "You are right, Elizabeth. Our perception of risk, irrespective of the real risk, reduces the more familiar we are with the situation. But I'll be very glad when we reach our destination and intend to get totally drunk before we return."

She then paid me a rather back-handed compliment.

"James, it is quite refreshing to hear a man display his

weaknesses in front of a woman. I think it takes courage. However, I would advise to go easy on the port if you are unaccustomed to it."

Needless to say, I did not take her advice.

The dinner party was for a friend's birthday and consisted of some of her class from school which enabled us to fabricate a suitable background. I posed as a University scicnce lecturer who was accompanying his sister on a literary tour. Jill was a great fan of Dickens, which gave her plenty of material on Victorian society, though I suggested she went easy on Ellen Ternan.

I quickly realised how ignorant we were when out of our time. I thought I knew a lot about Victorian society but it was like turning up at a party with no idea of the current pop groups or who was prime minister and having never heard of the '60s. There was nearly an uproar when I confused Gladstone with Disraeli; however, I saved myself with some knowledge of the recent Franco-Prussian War and I was glad to see that there was some sympathy for the French. They also listened quite intently on my view of the Prussians and how if they were not controlled a vast European war could ensue, though I did not mention expected casualties as I thought this would be beyond their credulity.

On a question regarding the English class system, Jill's rigorous defence of the 'undeserving' poor was not well received by everyone, though Elizabeth, at possibly some cost to herself, tried to support her. They were also quite surprised on how I had got into University without knowing a word of Latin. Chatting to the servants and thanking them for serving us caused some raised eyebrows as well; not least amongst the servants, who seemed quite embarrassed by our familiarity. I must also remember, after having half a bottle of port to follow the wine, not to try and explain what stars were made of to Victorians.

Elizabeth eventually saved us by "remembering" she had an early engagement in Chichester in the morning and we were able to leave before I caused any further trouble.

I don't remember the ride back to Hamgreen though later it became a favourite topic of conversation to be brought up by certain people.

---~---

E.

I was quite amazed how lacking our two new acquaintances were in matters of etiquette and their knowledge of Latin was almost non-existent. I felt a little embarrassed showing them how to use knives and forks in the correct order, but they were very interested and apologised profusely every time they made a mistake. James caused a little consternation, which I put down to the wine, by remarking it was the best Christmas dinner he had ever had. Jill quickly changed the subject by introducing the topic of favourite authors and I was surprised on how much she knew about Dickens and Elliott. James, when asked, regarded a Mr Sherlock Holmes as his favourite and was rather taken aback when we confessed that we had never heard of him.

Flory, who was beginning to suspect that his knowledge of English literature wasn't all that it should be for the best salons in Chichester, decided to test him on the Brontes and Austen. His reply regarding the 'affair' between Jane Eyre and Mr D'Arcy was received with much amusement to which Flory said rather devilishly, "Gosh Mr Urquhart, I must confess I must have skipped over those pages. I had not appreciated how racy those authors were."

Her friend Agnes, who with Flory had left a famous trail of broken hearts in the Bath season last year and could spot a weakened quarry at fifty yards, could not resist joining in by saying, "Perhaps your father removed the pages, Flory, so as not to offend your delicate soul."

I tried to interject before James noticed that the amusements were at his expense and his literary reputation was reduced completely to tatters, but his sister grabbed my hand and whispered, "Let it roll, Elizabeth. It pays back for all those times he has laughed at my ignorance in the area of science."

On poetry, however, he fared much better by entertaining us to Tam O'Shanter, helped I think by the port, and then redeemed himself completely by reciting two beautiful romantic poems by an Irish poet Mr Yates, which was so well received by the female company that he was made to promise to supply copies to all on his next visit. I thought he carried himself well in his frock coat and winged collars though when he asked to be more comfortable by removing his jacket I refused his request and reminded him it was a small price to pay compared to a lady's requirements to be fashionable. Then Flory, who thought she still had James well cornered, asked him for his opinion on marriage, to which he replied, parrying her foil quite cleverly I noted, by saying, "I believe it is intended to keep women out of mischief," and looked directly at Flory and Agnes, who both found a sudden interest in the remainder of their pudding.

"And," he said, giving a return thrust, "to get them in to trouble."

There was a sharp intake of breath but luckily, thanks to the beverage, this was judged to be just on the right side of decency and was well received by all save Flory and Agnes who now realised they had been 'found out' and that their quarry might be wilier than they thought. It also, more importantly deflected from any further questioning on the subject, for I had noticed one or two of my friends glancing between James and me in a surreptitious way. Later he told me this was the only "clean" Victorian joke he knew. I made a mental point to put him in touch with Henry and his chums to see who could outgun whom in this department, for I knew that although Henry would not recount any risqué humour with me, for some reason he was not so hesitant with Flory, who of course would delight in passing them on.

---~---

J.

On returning to our time after this rather embarrassing dinner party, I said to Jill, "I think we've got to improve our performance, some of them are beginning to suspect we are not quite what we are. My neck is raw from these starched collars and these trousers rub in all the wrong places. I think I'll go to the library and look up copies of the Gentleman's Magazine for the period to help us out."

"Do you really think some Victorian version of Men Only will help? I'm not convinced an afternoon of reading up on Victorian ladies' underwear is going to improve your amorous advances, Jim."

"It's what they called a Society Magazine, Jill. You know, a bit like Punch. And besides, from what you told me when they were here, I'd need the equivalent of a car maintenance manual, not a porn mag, to disassemble their clothes. Not, of course," noticing her look, "that I had any intention of doing so."

Mrs Beaton's Cookbook was very useful to help brush up on Victorian manners and Jill found 'A Gentleman's Guide to Etiquette' of 1875, which she thought would be of some use to me both in the present and the past. After a few attempts in engaging with each other in 'polite' conversation, she suggested that I pay close attention to the sections on buffoonery, phrases of double meaning and the use of inappropriate adjectives in the drawing room for some reason. Jill of course thoroughly enjoyed dressing up, though when I noticed she was going easy on the undergarments she said she wasn't going to let fashion get in the way of a good meal. However, she was soon able to converse knowledgeably on the latest ladies' fashion of the 1870s' bustles, flounces, corsets and polonaises, to which I tried to pay close attention.

I thought Elizabeth and Flory enjoyed our meetings and our 'little secret', though they would often tease by quizzing me on the latest scientific inventions and what I thought the future would hold. This invariably led me into using technical words which required a lot of stumbling about, much to the amusement of her friends who eventually began to regard me as a bit of an eccentric. This was compounded by Jill who, I later found out, had also shown them my book on Gentlemen's Etiquette and they had derived much amusement at my expense in counting how many of the 37 rules I could break in one sitting! As Rule 16 prohibits the use of derogatory comments on those who are absent, I will say no more.

---~---

E.

On two occasions James brought Flory and me back to his own time. This was more difficult for us. We had some understanding of the past, but we had never seen the future. There was so much that was completely new: television, telephones, computers, the distance we could travel so easily and of course aeroplanes – every time we heard one, we would rush out into the garden and gaze with awe and excitement at the white pencil trails disappearing towards the horizon. We were especially amazed by the amount of money they had and why they didn't have servants and a bigger house, until we saw the ridiculous cost of everything. Flory tried to relate the cost to our own time and reckoned that the amount of money we had in trust for life would be spent in three months here.

I had become much interested in their clothes and enquired of Jill of what material her dresses were made. She said they were made from an artificial substance called 'Lycra', which was apparently a girl's best friend, allowing her 'to pig out', as she put it, without discomfort at any dinner party. I said I must admit at one or two fine dinner parties I had attended I'd wished my clothes had been made of such a material to allow me to 'pig out' as well. However, when I asked her who her haberdasher was, she replied that she bought from an awfully nice company which employed small children in India and China to make them for a tuppence an hour. I told her that was very charitable of her as I had heard there was much poverty and starvation in the empire and to hear that she subscribed to a firm which paid such a generous wage to these poor people was very noble.

One evening they took us into Chichester to what they called an Italian restaurant, though the decor seemed to be English peasant vernacular rather than renaissance. We enjoyed it. We had what I believe they called 'Pizza', which is like a large flat unleavened bread filled with melted cheeses, spices and meats and was delicious, though eating it with our hands took some getting used to. It was very informal. No one wore evening dress and we were very surprised that the serving staff would join in our conversations unasked.

While we were there a group of young ladies entered, who by the state of their attire looked like they had had to leave a house suddenly in the middle of the night due to a fire and had spent the evening, judging by their gait and coarse merriment, wandering around Chichester in a state of such distress that they had drunk copious amounts of liquor to alleviate their situation. I was quite shocked when Jill told me this was a Hen Party and it was traditional for ladies to dress and carry on in this fashion the day before they were married. I can only presume in their houses they were not blessed with any mirrors to regard themselves. Some it seemed, by their age and application of paint, were obviously their mothers, who should have been ashamed of themselves and known better than to ape their daughters. I made a mental note that when I marry it would be in my own time, though why that thought came into my mind I am not quite sure.

I noticed while eating that one waiter seemed to take a particular fancy to Flory and without any ceremony started to flirt with her. I had never seen her blush so much. I looked at James for assistance but he just smiled and winked at me, which I took as assurance that no harm would come to her. He was right, though at the end of the evening as we were leaving the waiter came over to Flory, bowed, kissed her hand and presented her with a single red rose! Then he was off without an adieu to serve other customers! Later Jill told me that Italian waiters were all the same and mostly harmless. They reminded me of the German waiters in the cafés around Leicester Square who would spare no expense in flattering single ladies. However, Flory was quite affected for some time and had difficulty accepting that what she thought was a proposal was not genuine.

---~---

J.
I was glad that they enjoyed our company and were

beginning to be relaxed with our manners. Jill and I did try to be as formal as we could without laughing too much, but if they noticed us poking fun they usually got their own back in their own period by showing up our manners in front of their friends.

One evening they asked to us to describe what had come to pass in the world since their time. Jill and I tried to make a timeline using YouTube clips on the telly, showing the world leaders and events through the 20th century. They were absolutely gobsmacked with the first landing on the moon.

But what shocked them completely was war. In this land of seemingly plenty for everyone, the endless wars; the huge scales of death; the weapons, the nukes. The saw their own future in the twentieth century and what was in store for their own children and grandchildren. I think they knew that human wars were endless, they were well read and not naive in their outlook or knowledge, but Elizabeth summed up the unease it gave them.

"You know, James, I realise things do not change and there will always be evil and malady, but I do feel that it is better not to know the future because then there is hope. To be presented with the reality of what is unavoidably to come to oneself is not something with which we can become comfortable. It takes away what we might call our free will."

Then one day it came to an end. The planned engagements failed to materialise. There was no answer on the phone. I feared the worst, death, illness, even marriage. I didn't even know what time she was in. She could be wandering around lost in my era unable to get home. I scanned through the local papers. Nothing. Jill just stopped me in time from phoning the police to report a missing person by pointing out how the conversation might go.

Me: Hello, I want to report a missing woman.
Police: Where does she live?
Me: In 1873 she lived in Hamgreen Lodge but not now.
Police: So sir, if I may take it that she's not alive now sir, have you tried the Registry Office?
Me: No, I mean she is alive now but someone else is living in her house now.
Police: So sir, if she doesn't live there now, where does she live?
Me: When she's here she stays with me.
Police: And where does she live when she is not staying with you?
Me: Hamgreen Lodge of course.
Police: So sir, if I understand you correctly, this missing person, who seems to be over 140 years old, used to live in Hamgreen but now lives with you except when she doesn't, when she lives in Hamgreen where she doesn't live anymore. Have we been partaking in alcoholic beverages or recreational substances, sir?

Not being able to think up a better story that didn't end up bringing the men in white coats around we tried the county records at Chichester of the 1870s to see if we could find anything. Jill, having saved me from a life of psychiatric care, reminded me that if Elizabeth or Flory approached the Victorian authorities with the same story they would be locked up in no time. We looked through the inmates of the Sussex lunatic asylums. Nothing, though in those days, I imagined they could have just been locked up in an attic somewhere.

We eventually found her. It was a newspaper clipping. A Miss Bicester had left the lodge at Hamgreen to visit her aunt in Chichester but never returned. The paper noted that the subsequent search and investigation did not discover any aunt, though her driver and maid swore they had dropped her off at a small cottage in Chichester and seen her enter the premises. Further investigation revealed no aunt living at the cottage, only an old couple who had never heard of Elizabeth.

This, as Jill quickly reminded me, indicated Elizabeth had come back to our future because we knew the 'aunt' was Elizabeth's fabrication for her first visit to us.

But we had still not got to the bottom of the time shift. Why just us and no one else? It only occurred at certain events where Elizabeth had said people were there who had been present at the cricket club.

I decided to search for records of her cousin's cricket team at the archives. I eventually found them, the Lord Fotheringale's Eleven. I then spent time looking through the Chichester archives, in the announcement pages of the local papers and magazines, looking for their names in engagements that Elizabeth was expected to attend. We found five with members of Lord Fotheringale Eleven in attendance, and three of the members appeared at each event, including her cousin Henry.

"So where does this get us, Jim?"

"I was hoping something would stand out."

"There is something. Look at this photo here of the cricket team. The one third from the left."

"What?"

"Look. Mr Cambio D'Ora. The one holding the cricket bat."

"Doesn't look very different from the others, same clothes ..."

"Look at his bat. It's got a wide flat edge to it."

"So?"

"That's a modern bat. Didn't come in till about the '70s."

"How do you know that?"

"You'd be surprised what men show me when they invite me back for coffee".

I let that one pass and quickly and came up with nothing but a list of Italian websites.

"Nothing much here. Wait, how about this – cambiata l'ora."

"That looks close. What does it mean?"

"It means ... according to this web dictionary, my god! 'Changed time'!"

"Let me see. Oh, you're right Jim. That's too much of a coincidence."

I looked up the variant on Google but no one of that name came up. I tried 1870, 1880. Still nothing.

"OK, he's playing games. It's too obvious. Maybe it's an anagram."

After a while all we could come up with was Marco.

"Maybe we should rearrange the phrase you found on Google."

I took the phrase 'cambiata l'ora' and removed Marco and rearranging the remaining letters came up with Batalia ... Marco Batalia.

We looked at each other. Then we both grabbed our tablets and started googling Marco Batalia.

"I've found him!" said Jill, "He's a lecturer at Manchester University. It must be him or we will have to admit we have gone completely bonkers!"

"What's his subject?"

"Astrophysics."

"Well that's the right subject. It's full of stuff on space-time. If it is him we need to get him to reveal himself. I have seen nothing in the journals on time travel."

"Maybe we should call his bluff by pretending we are Elizabeth and her cousin Henry."

"Or, I just tell him I'm James Urquhart because when I told Elizabeth and her cousin my name I had the distinct impression my name was already known to them."

"My god, does that mean you were there before you met Elizabeth and Flory?"

"If I was it hasn't happened yet ... if you get what you mean."

"But what did you do to become so infamous?"

"There is only one way to find out."

I picked up the phone and phoned Manchester. A secretary answered and said that Mr Batalia was not available but if I left my name and number she would get him to phone me back. I took the chance and gave her my name.

Half an hour later the phone rang. I picked it up.

"Mr Urquhart?"

"Yes."

"What can I do for you?"

If he was our man he was playing it cool. I played my only ace.

"Mr Cambio D'Ora?"

There was silence. Then,

"Mr Urquhart, we need to talk. Can you come up to Manchester? I am in the new building next to the Rutherford Laboratory."

The next morning we were on our way to Manchester Uni. I took the M6 toll road to avoid Spaghetti Junction. We got into Oxford Street about one and went to the laboratory reception. Mr Batalia was waiting for us. He was wearing a close-fitting grey collarless suit and zipped shirt and had the air of one of those Silicon Valley whizz kids who had made his pile. His accent was that global English of the much-travelled man, though there was an undertone which suggested that it was not his first language. He took us into the canteen and was good enough to treat us to lunch, where he quizzed us on our time-travelling adventures.

"So it seems," he said, "You just walked into this field and there you were in 1873 in the middle of cricket match?"

"Yes, but the interesting thing is that her cousin already knew my name."

"That's because you had already been there two years before in 1871."

"How do you know?"

"Because I met you there."

"But what? How? I haven't been there yet."

"Correct."

We looked totally baffled.

"So you see I have to send you back there."

"You mean if I don't go none of what's happened will happen?"

"Exactly. In fact, I need both of you to make it work."

"So how? Do you have a time machine?"

"Yes, of sorts."

I looked around. There was nothing I recognised as a time machine, not that I had any idea what one looked like, except the Tardis, of course.

"The problem is that in order to join me I have to join my time nodes to yours."

We looked very puzzled.

"Look, each of us travels along our own time line at the speed of light. Not slower or faster. If you stand still you travel at that speed."

"Yes, but if you start to move, you will go faster than light."

"No Mr Urquhart. Time will slow down to compensate. But there is something else. Note you can only meet Elizabeth at exactly the same time of the year. You can't meet the day before or the next day simply because the earth won't be there to meet you. It's moved through its own space time. You, by the way, Mr Urquhart, cleverly deduced this by asking for her engagements."

"Yes, but going back over 100 years the sun would have moved as well."

"I know, I am having difficulty with that. What could be happening is that nodes or resonances have been set up along our time lines and at each of these nodes our time lines are somehow tethered to each other and allow us to oscillate between them at certain times of the year."

"But," I said, "why just 1873 and 1871? And more importantly what is the connection between Elizabeth and me?"

"I don't know. There may be other dates we don't know about yet. These oscillations could be happening all the time which construct into resonances. Perhaps in most cases they are momentary and people do not even detect the time difference. Most of them may just exist for just a few seconds."

"But we have been together sometimes for hours."

Marco thought about this.

"Maybe it's like gluons."

"What?"

"You know, the things that exchange between fundamental particles and keep them bound together. So as long as you are interacting with the other time node, the longer you stay. As soon as you move away, the nodes break apart. Hey, I could call them 'timeons' or 'chronons'."

"Chronons! Do they exist?"

"No idea, but Zweig invented his quark long before it was found, and as for Higgs, they didn't find his god particle for over 40 years. I could be on the lecture gravy train for years."

"Ok Einstein, but what about the phone calls?" Jill said, "There are no mobile transmitters in 1873."

"I know. But radio waves travel at the speed of light. So they only travel through space, they do not travel through time. You know light doesn't shine on something unless it has something to shine on. I mean a light ray or radio wave takes no time to travel from one object to another but also more importantly it won't travel to the other object unless it knows it is there."

"So how does it know it is there?" Said Jill.

"Eh? Oh, it only knows it is there because it is already connected."

"So", I said with the beginning of headache, "Somehow my phone is connected to me!"

"Well," said Jill, "that would explain it. I always thought Jim's phone was surgically attached to him in some way."

"Correct. So in order for you to come with me I have to ..."

"Connect to our time line!" I interrupted, beginning to see his point.

"No, Mr Urquhart, your timeline can't join mine. But I think I can fool it by putting you both in stasis so you are invisible in mine and could move through my timeline undetected."

"How you going to do that?"

"The electromagnetic fields of your timeline must be contained."

"How?"

"We start with schoolboy physics. We put you in a Faraday cage."

"But from what I can remember those only stop electric fields. What about the magnetic component of the radiation or even the earth's magnetic field?"

"I'm trying all the tricks. Copper for RF and mu-metal for

slowly changing magnetic fields like the Earth's."

"Mmh. You've obviously put some thought into this. Do you know what you are doing?"

"Haven't a clue. All I know is that this time travel is happening."

"So what do we do in 1871?"

"We go to Urquhart Castle."

"What, the one in Scotland?"

Jill looked at me in mock surprise, "I didn't know we had a castle, Jim."

"You don't," said Marco, "It might have belonged to your ancestors once but those days are long gone."

"So how is our surname linked to this castle now?"

"I don't know. But it might just be another contribution to strengthening the node resonances."

"Ok, so what do we do at our ancestors' castle?"

"First we go to the hunting lodge at Brachla near the Loch where we will meet Elizabeth's cousin Henry."

"And how do you know that?"

"Because I meet you there that day with Henry's shooting party."

I mentally put my hands up in surrender.

"And why do I need to see Henry?"

"Because he told me at Hamgreen Cricket Club, the day you were there, that he had just met some scruffy individual talking to his sister who claimed to be the James Urquhart whom he had met in Scotland at his shooting party and he had good reason to know that it could not be true. Luckily, he pointed you out to me and I could immediately tell from your clothes you were out of your time and when you got your phone out that clinched it. By the way, what did you actually say to the Bicester sisters?"

I decided to let that one pass.

"So to preserve the continuity I have to meet him in Scotland in 1871?"

"Yes, and if we don't do this everything could collapse."

"When is it going to happen?"

"I don't know exactly", he said, "Which means there is some urgency in preparing you for your trip back to 1871."

"And how you going to hide such a stasis box containing me and my sister in 1871?"

"Come and see. I have had an excellent idea."

He took us into an adjoining laboratory.

"My god!' I said, "How much did that cost?"

He turned with a grin –"It's amazing what you can raise through crowd sourcing if you target the right audience."

---~---

Out of Time

Chapter Four

E.

Life had returned almost to normal for Flory and me, but I could not get him out of my mind.

"I've been thinking, Flory, about James' first appearance."

"Really Elizabeth, I thought you had completely forgotten about him."

"Do not tease, Flory. You remember Henry was quite taken aback when he met James?"

"Yes, Elizabeth. I was quite shocked by his manner. You think it is not a coincidence that Henry knew the name?"

"I think, Flory, we should go and talk to our cousin to see what he knows."

"Yes, and question him closely. I believe he is staying up at Lurgashall; we will send a messenger ahead to tell him we are coming to visit."

When we arrived he was waiting on the drive. Henry had obviously just been out shooting because he was still wearing an old sack jacket and his favourite baggy green cord trousers which he wore for a bit of "rabbiting" or, as Flory called it, shooting little defenceless furry animals with a blunderbuss. He took us in without removing his muddy boots and treated us to an afternoon tea. It was what I would call a typical gentleman's house. Antlers on the walls, paintings of race horses, tableaux of game forlornly laid out on kitchen tables and a faint lingering smell of stale cigar. Its permanent fixture was Jennings, a retired butler, who each morning decanted a large sherry for visitors in the hall and retrieved it about teatime. This was known as 'Jennings' Jolly' and if visitors wished to have any cooperation from him they were advised to leave the 'Jolly' alone.

"So, what brings my cousins all the way up here? I'm certain it's not for the shoot," said my cousin.

"Well Henry, we want to know what you know about James Urquhart."

He frowned, got up and paced the room for a few moments glancing at us now and then as if he were trying to make up his mind. Then he turned and sat down next to us. I noticed his moustache was rather asymmetrical, indicating he had once again been attempting to cut a new style with limited success. Then looking straight at me he said, "Have you ever heard of the Loch Ness Monster?"

"Why yes, Henry. It must appear in the magazines every year at the commencement of the tourist season in Scotland."

"Precisely, a little publicity for the curious and gullible. However, I have seen it."

"What!"

"Yes, I was staying at a hunting lodge two years ago by Loch Ness with a shooting party."

"I did not know there were any grouse left in Scotland, Henry?"

"I will ignore that, Flory. Anyway, while we were there, a Mr James Urquhart arrived with that Italian fellow."

"Who, Henry?" I exclaimed.

"You know, the Italian fellow, Mr Cambio D'Ora, the one who lives up at Midhurst. Nice chap and seemed very knowledgeable on stars and planets and that sort of thing. Claimed he knew that chap Biddle Airy who made Greenwich the meridian for the whole world remember?"

"Do not tease Henry. You said you met Mr James Urquhart!"

"Yes. The real one, not the impersonator we met at the Cricket Club."

I did not understand. James had said that our encounter at the cricket club was his first experience in our time. Yet Henry plainly had just said he had seen him, or someone with the same name? Two years before!

"So Henry, what happened? I mean with your encounter with this Mr Urquhart?"

"The next morning we took the carriages to see the ruins of Urquhart Castle on the Loch. I enquired if Mr Urquhart was related to the Urquhart clan but he was quite unknowledgeable on the whole subject and seemed decidedly unsure of himself in the matter.

"Anyway, we eventually climbed to the top of the ruin. It was a bright sunny day and of course we were all hoping to see the Loch Ness monster and suddenly there it was!"

"What, you saw it? Did James, I mean Mr Urquhart, did he take a photograph with his phone?"

"Pardon, Elizabeth?"

"Sorry Henry, I was getting too involved with your story. Did he have a small black case which he pointed at the creature?"

"Why, yes he did, Elizabeth! How did you know? He was very excited and held it in front of himself for some time. Then he did a most peculiar thing. He pressed it, then holding it to his ear, began to talk into it! We thought he must be having a brain fever. I have seen men, whom you would think were the sturdiest kind, lose their nerves in unfamiliar circumstances. But I thought he had gone completely mad because he started walking down to the creature."

"Oh my god! What did the creature do?"

"Nothing at first. It was big, about twenty feet long and black all over. There was what looked like a large fin on top and one on its tail. It had two large black slits above its nose which I took to be its eyes. But then it moved towards the shore and its mouth, which I had not noticed before, opened and Mr Urquhart, before we could stop him, walked straight into its mouth which closed immediately and the creature slowly sank beneath the water!"

"Oh Flory! He has been eaten! What a tragedy! We have lost him. We will never see him again."

Flory held my hand and came close to whisper, "Elizabeth! Calm yourself. Remember?"

"Remember what?"

"We saw James two years after this event. He must be alive. By some means he must have escaped!"

Henry looked at us incredulously.

"Are you suggesting, Flory, that the man you both introduced to me at the cricket club was not an imposter but was actually this chap Urquhart?"

"Yes, Henry. And that is why we asked you about the black case and the photographs. He had such as device at Hamgreen. In fact, I still have it."

"My god!"

"Yes, my dear cousin, and now we understand why you were so shocked to see him."

"No, Elizabeth. I don't mean that, I mean you said you have his black case!"

"Oh yes Henry, we have communicated many times."

Henry slowly sat down.

I suddenly realised we had overstepped the mark. We possibly had a lot of explaining to do. Much of which would possibly require defending our honour and reputations quite vigorously.

---∼---

J.

It was a dark grey green, over twenty feet long and shaped

like a cigar. There was no obvious entrance but when Marco pressed a mark on the hull the front slowly opened like a mouth.

"Welcome to the Loch Ness Monster". He said with the smile of someone showing off a new toy. "This is where the legend starts Mr Urquhart. Do you want to go in?"

"After you", I said.

We followed Marco up the ramp and into the mouth. The inside was almost empty save for a chair and a console. It was illuminated by a suffused red glow which seemed to emanate from the hull walls.

The mechanism was simple: one joystick, an Xbox controller and a simple cam connected to a video screen. For communication Marco had set up a Wi-Fi transmitter and receiver on the boat which linked to my new phone.

"Ok, Mr Urquhart. If it works then you should find yourselves in the Loch near Urquhart Castle in 1871."

"What do you mean IN the Loch?"

"Don't worry. It's waterproof. It's good down to about a hundred feet. If you find yourselves below the surface just use these controls, like this to raise it. Make sure it's on the surface though before you open the door. Anyway, good luck. I'll meet you there". And he left us.

"James? What are we doing?"

"I don't know Jill. For all I know he's locked us in and thrown away the key".

We both rushed for the door. It was locked.

"God Jim. We must be bloody idiots. We are now locked in a box with no idea of escape. We're going to die aren't we?"

For some reason I couldn't think of a reassuring answer.

We must have waited, watching the screen for over an hour when suddenly we noticed the moon.

"It's happened Jill."

"What's happened Jim?"

I moved the Cam around. I could see we were on water and above there were stars.

"It looks like we're on Loch Ness, Jill. I can just see the castle. Move this monster forwards slowly towards it if you can."

There was a sudden lurch forward.

"Bloody hell Jill. Careful!"

"Sorry Jim. Perhaps the one who spends his evening on his games machine in his 'shed' pretending he's marking papers would be better at it."

I must remember to keep that attic door closed and use head phones in future.

Then the stasis box. hit the shoreline with a mild crunch and stopped.

"I think we've landed. OK, let's open the door and get out before it sinks."

I opened the bow. Marco was standing on the castle embankment.

"Hello," I said. "I'm Jim Urquhart and this is ..."

"Yes, I know."

"But you said this is the first time we met or, er, meet."

"Yes, along the timeline. But you see I seem to be stuck not only in a time loop but a memory loop as well. I am meeting you here for the first time coming out the stasis box, but I already know that in the future we build the stasis box to come back here. And in the future I already know we have met here. My brain is unable to think which came first. In this time loop the memories of our two meetings are joined in a circle. It just goes around and around. There is no first encounter."

"Jeez! And you're hoping this will get you out of the loop. OK, so what do we do now?"

"Well, James, you come with me. Jill, I'm afraid you have to stay in the stasis box till tomorrow."

"What?" She said.

"It's OK, there is food and drink in a case at the back."

"And if I need a pee?"

"Ah. I forgot. You'll have to use the bucket."

"Oh thanks very much! You go off to your soirée while I spend the night in a black box on a bucket!"

We tried to look suitably embarrassed.

"I've got no choice, have I? Oh, she'd better be worth it James!"

And she closed the bow door and slowly submerged below the water.

We walked along the track to the hunting lodge.

"So, Marco, how did you get into their cricket team?"

"Oh, that was easy. I played juniors for Sussex and also Manchester Uni. Henry's eleven haven't a clue, you know. Imagine the advantage with all the coaching I've had access to."

"No, I mean, how did you get involved with them in the first place? Do you have a time machine?"

"Not at the time. It was like you. One day I was in the clubhouse at Midhurst. When I came out to play in my cricket gear, there I was in 1870."

"What did they say?"

"They didn't. No one noticed, including me at first. I just walked up to the crease and whacked off six sixes in a row. Never seen such bad bowling. After that I was Fotheringale's Eleven's best mate. It wasn't till I got back to the club house that I realised I didn't recognise anyone and they discovered that no one owned up to knowing me."

"What happened?"

"I bluffed. I said I must have turned up at the wrong game and hadn't noticed. Well, they were not daft. They decided that my performance far outweighed my story and immediately asked me to join their club."

"So, when did you realise you were out of your time?"

"Luckily, fairly quickly when I returned to the club house. Their clothes, manners and servants, not to mention their incredulous attention to my kit, helmet and bat gave me the clue. So by the time they quizzed me on my background I was ready for them. I told them I was an amateur astronomer, which went down extremely well and wasn't far from the truth."

We had arrived at the hunting lodge. We went up to the main entrance and introduced ourselves to the porter, saying we had got lost on the moors and wondered if we could stay overnight.

It wasn't long before Henry appeared, who seemed very affable and once he heard my name wanted to know everything about the Urquhart Clan. I wish I had taken more interest in my granddad's ancestors. Henry's group were having a day off from shooting the next day and said they were going to explore the castle ruins. We said it was on our way and they kindly invited us to join them.

Now everything depended on Jill.

When we arrived at the castle the next morning we climbed up the ruins to get a view of the Loch. As we all looked over the wall I texted a signal to Jill to raise the boat. It worked like a dream. Complete mayhem. The whole shooting party were in uproar. I took some photos of the fun and then signalled Jill to open the bow door. As it opened I slowly walked down the hill and calmly walked into the Loch Ness Monster submarine, hoping not to catch the contents of a bucket.

Jill closed the doors.

"Brilliant, Jill."

"Yeah, and thanks for asking how I got through the night with only a bucket for a friend."

I realised this was another lose-lose situation.

"Ok, I'm an unfeeling bastard but let's quietly submerge and get out of here. We'll be all over the papers by the weekend. I can see it all – the well-known eccentric Mr James Urquhart was swallowed by the Loch Ness Monster – read all about it."

"Yes Jim, and if I see an old picture of me squatting on a bucket in the archives you're a dead man. However, there's just one problem."

"What?"

"How do we get back?"

"Damn!"

---~---

E.

"So Elizabeth," said Henry, looking me straight in the eye when we had finished our explanations. I had purposely left out our difference in time. Mainly because I had no idea how to explain it or to give concrete proof of its existence. While we all thought Mr Urquhart was just an eccentric member of your aunt's staff he was actually also your lover."

"How dare you, Henry! You will not spread that rumour. At no time was I ever on my own with Mr Urquhart. I am well aware that I have my reputation to protect and you should know that I would not put myself in a compromising position."

"Ah yes, but perhaps you may have thought of putting yourself in, as you put it, a compromising position."

"Well, really!" And I stamped out of the room and slammed the door. I was pleased to hear my sister giving him such a tongue lashing that I was sure he would take some time to forget it.

After a couple of minutes the door opened and my cousin appeared a little sheepishly.

"I feel I must apologise, Elizabeth, for questioning your reputation. Your sister has done more than enough to convince me that even questioning in half-jest on this subject was extremely rude of me."

"Well, it is alright for you, Henry, gallivanting about with your friends, but it is very difficult for a lady to have fun and keep a reputation that will still make her eligible for a suitable engagement or marriage."

"You are quite right, Elizabeth. I do feel we men sometimes put women on too high a pedestal and then admonish them for falling off."

"I can assure you I have no intention of falling off my pedestal, as you say."

"Ah yes, Elizabeth, but I have observed many a lady purposely fall off her pedestal, if you allow me to continue to labour the euphemism, if the right gentleman passes by to catch her."

He had seen through me very easily and he could see that I followed his drift, but he was kind enough not to pursue it.

"So, Elizabeth," he said, putting his hand gently on my knee, which I removed immediately, "How are we going to find your Mr Urquhart again?"

"Thank you, Henry, for understanding our situation. I have his black case and he has a list of my engagements, but he has failed to appear at the last three."

"But we have a link, Elizabeth. Mr D'Ora at Midhurst. Remember I first met him with Mr Urquhart at Loch Ness?"

"Of course! We must go to him at once."

"Steady. It is getting late. I will send a messenger post haste. Write a quick note, Elizabeth, about you and Mr Urquhart and ask how you might meet him again."

I did not feel confident enough to do such a thing but I did not want to reveal my feelings.

"As we have been discussing the preservation of my reputation, Henry, I would prefer that you wrote on my behalf. I do not want to look too forward."

"You are quite right, Elizabeth, if you look too forward you might fall off your pedestal without your Mr Urquhart to catch you."

My pocketbook caught him nicely on the side of the forehead.

---~---

J.

"So, Jim, what do we do?" said Jill.

"We wait."

"Oh great, and second prize is, two nights in a sealed tub accompanied by one thunder box and a lousy brother. And suppose we run out of air?"

"We just surface and open the hatch."

"And now death by drowning. Are all your dates like this, Jim? Don't answer that. Oh well, what have we got to lose? Let's chance it."

We slowly raised the boat until the camera was above water.

"Oh my god! There are boats everywhere! Damn! One of them has seen us. Dive, Jill!"

We slowly went down. I remember reading somewhere that Loch Ness was very deep, so we should be able to hide easily, except suddenly the hull began to creek alarmingly. I had not asked Marco what pressure it could stand. Not that it mattered because there was no pressure gauge.

Suddenly the noise stopped. We looked at each other.

"Raise it slowly to the surface, Jill. I'll watch the cam."

Nothing happened. The cam display was black.

We waited for about half an hour. Nothing moved.

"Do you think we've run aground?"

"I can't tell."

"Maybe we have returned to the lab?"

"There's only one way to find out. Open the hatch."

"What?! No way, Jim!"

I looked at the hatch door. Then I noticed Marco's crowd-sourcing had funded a tell-tale.

"It's got a tell-tale, Jill. All I have to do is open this tap. If there is no water then there is no water outside."

I turned the tap. It was dry. Unfortunately at the moment I remembered an article on HMS Thetis, which sunk because someone had filled the tell-tale pipe with paint. I decided to keep that to myself and to go ahead anyway. I convinced Jill to open the door, and she was no doubt spurred on by another night in the box. With a creak it slowly opened. Water dripped around the seal.

"Keep going, Jill."

The door continued to open; no further water came in. When it was fully open I looked out. It was pitch black outside. I climbed out, feeling for the ground. Relief! It was a wooden floor. We were back in the lab.

I turned on a light. The lab was empty.

"So what do we do now, Jim?"

"I've no idea. Find Marco?"

---∼---

E.

The messenger returned just before bedtime. He had found

Mr D'Ora out so he gave it to his neighbour, who promised to deliver it as soon as he returned.

The next morning after breakfast a servant announced there was a Mr Cambio D'Ora to see me and that he apologised for not coming sooner. I immediately invited him to join me in the breakfast room. He was wearing rather old-fashioned clothes which looked surprisingly new. I realised he had got the year's fashion wrong, but I said nothing.

"Good morning, Mr D'Ora. Thank you for coming so quickly. As you know, we are hoping you could help us find Mr James Urquhart."

"Yes I can, madam. Everything has been a success."

He smiled at me with a look that indicated James had given him a favourable impression of my character.

"What do we do now, Mr D'Ora?"

"I'm afraid that is now up to you, Miss Bicester."

I was afraid. "What do you mean?"

"I mean the time loop is complete, you have one chance and only one chance of seeing Mr Urquhart again."

"And then?"

"It depends on your decision."

"Please be plainer, Mr D'Ora! I am not quite myself, as you might imagine."

"I know, Miss Bicester. I mean Mr Urquhart can no longer come to you but you can go to him."

"And how long can I see him for?"

"As long as you like. But if you come back here the time window will close and you will not see him again."

"And where is he now?"

"He is with your 'aunt' in Chichester."

"And if I wished to do such a thing, when would I have to make my decision?

He looked me straight in the eyes. "Now, Miss Bicester."

I could almost feel that window closing as he spoke those words.

---~---

J.

We arrived back in Chichester and looked up Marco's number in Midhurst. He answered.

"Thank god you're back." He said. "It means it has all worked."

"What has worked?"

"It means I can meet up with Miss Bicester and bring her back if you want her. Or more importantly if she wants you."

I looked at Jill.

"Well, Jim, judgement day has arrived. Do I phone all my girlfriends and tell them that you've stopped chasing around or do I tell them to continue to keep their doors locked?"

It was no contest.

"And when do I have to make this decision, Marco?"

"Now."

"And how long can she stay?"

"If she comes, forever. I expect your time nodes will then break. I cannot believe they will ever join again."

---~---

E.

Mr Ora and I found Henry and Flora in the morning drawing room and explained that I needed to visit my aunt in Chichester where I should also find James. "What do you think, Henry?"

"I do not quite understand the urgency, but I think you must go with Mr D'Ora. He is obviously in earnest."

"On my own, without a chaperone, Henry? What about my reputation?"

"Of course, Elizabeth. I'd almost forgotten you had one."

Before I could respond in an appropriate fashion he said, "I suggest you take my carriage and one of the maids and follow Mr D'Ora. I would suggest Flory accompanies you but I think you two share too many secrets for your own good."

Flory was studiously looking at a piece of needlework on her lap.

"Thank you, Henry. Then I will take up Mr D'Ora's offer."

I looked at Flory and she looked at me and then we both embraced each other.

We followed Mr D'Ora down to Chichester in Henry's carriage and arrived at the cottage where Flory and I had previously stayed with James and his sister. I alighted from the carriage and walked up to the porch. I heard the sound of a carriage behind me and turned just in time to see Mr D'Ora drive off. Thankfully my carriage was still waiting there. I turned, knocked three times on the door and waited.

After a moment it opened and there was James.

---~---

J.

There was a gentle knock at the door. Was it Marco or Elizabeth? I looked at Jill.

"Jim, I don't envy you. What will you do if she is standing there?"

"Part of me will use all the strength in my body to send her back."

"And the other part?"

"It will use all my guile and wit to keep her."

She looked me in the eye briefly then came up very close to me and whispered, "Just open the door, Jim."

I went into the hall. I turned the lock and opened the front door. There she was. She was dressed in the powder blue I had seen at the Priory Park and she was carrying a large, embroidered bag.

I opened the door wider. Then with only a brief hesitation she crossed the threshold.

---~---

Out of Time

Chapter Five

J.

We stood in the hallway opposite each other in silence.

Then I noticed Jill was giving me a look indicating that this historic romantic interchange between two persons separated by over 100 years was not quite up to the standard Jane Austen would expect, and interjected, "I think I need to rearrange the cacti in the conservatory." And disappeared into the kitchen.

Elizabeth looked at me.

"Mr Urquhart, I did not know you had a conservatory."

"We don't, Miss Bicester. Nor do we have any cacti."

"Ah, I see."

I suddenly felt her vulnerability. She had left her time, on her own, with no turning back.

"Shall we go into the living room?' I said.

She hesitated. Jill had started making washing up noises in the kitchen and had turned the radio on.

Then she followed me in.

"Elizabeth?"

"Yes, James."

"As you well know I am sometimes a little more forward than you wish me to be, but I assure you I have no wish to offend you. So if I do, will you promise to tell me?"

"I will, James."

"I wish to ask you a question which I hope will not offend. May I?"

I could see she stiffened a little.

"You can, James, if it is within reason."

"Then ... may I kiss you?"

She took a sharp intake of breath then her body relaxed. "Yes, you may, James"

She came to me. She smelt of musk and oranges.

---～---

E.

I did not expect to be alone with him so soon and I certainly did not expect his proposition but his hesitance in delivery, so contrary to his usual confidence, reassured me. His manner by which he stole a kiss was also, I must admit, well played and to my liking and I began to realise that despite the lack of formal manners he was obviously not unsophisticated. He also drew away a moment sooner than I wished, which I liked, and caressed my cheek before dropping his hand to mine. This caused me to respond by quickly kissing him on his cheek, as a way of thank you, which when he saw my surprised look made us both laugh.

However, I was now unsure of what etiquette in his time required and in truth I found I was unsure of mine. I looked to him for help.

---～---

J.

I could see we were at an impasse. I suddenly realised that we were both constrained by our own worlds and needed to understand each other's conventions. Time for a break.

"Well, Elizabeth. I think we should go and help my sister with her cacti."

"Yes, James. But I must be careful not to prick myself."

And she gave me a smile with her eyes which took me back to our first meeting when I thought I saw a door within was now ajar.

We went into the kitchen. Jill had her best "I'm not curious" face on. And then devilishly said, "Oh Jim, have you been making pastry?"

"Pardon?"

"You seem to have some flour on you."

I betrayed myself by instantly feeling my cheek and found a trace of white powder. Elizabeth blushed.

"Dear Elizabeth," said Jill, "you must borrow some of my cosmetics. They are very helpful in preserving our honour."

"Thank you, Jill, but you must remember that in my time a lady wearing paint, if that is what you mean, would have difficulty being regarded with any honour."

Touché, I thought and sided with Elizabeth.

"Jill," I said, "that's not fair. How would you like it if you were transported back to 1873 on your own dressed as you are?"

"Point taken, Jim. I'm sorry Elizabeth. Sisters, eh?"

"You are certainly right Jill, and don't talk to me about cousins. I am often surprised what Flory knows about me and what my cousin Henry thinks about me.

Then Jill changed the subject with a better offer.

"Anyway Elizabeth, now that you are here. I have a treat for you. We go to Chi tomorrow. First to book you in to my hairdressers then we will shop 'til we drop at Jim's expense."

"What?" I said.

"You owe me for that night in the tub, remember?"

I had wondered when that would come up again.

"OK, fair enough, but I'm coming with you to see what you are buying."

"Jim, you do know we only buy clothes to impress other women. Don't we, Elizabeth?"

"Why, yes, Jill, but I would not give away too many of our feminine secrets. We have so few. Remember, James, it is other women who are always our competition." And her eyes darted momentarily from me to my sister.

The next morning after an hour in Chi, I was dispatched to

Waterstones where I spent most of the day out of harm's way skimming through crap bestsellers and drinking coffee.

It seems I was inexplicably 'caught' in Mark & Sparks lingerie section and then unjustly 'accused' of examining items which I might have thought appropriate for Elizabeth.

---~---

E.

My first impression of this new Chichester was its cleanliness, the absence of the odour of coal smoke and the taste of windblown dried horse manure so prevalent on hot days. The buildings had been scrubbed clean of soot and were gleaming white. Refuse, carts, horses, street vendors and urchins had vanished, allowing me to peruse the shops uninterrupted. The uniformity of the fashions was puzzling though, as it made it difficult to distinguish one class from another. Medical advances must have been miraculous as there was almost a complete absence of cripples and beggars. Later, after we had packed James off to a cafeteria for what Jill and I thought was inappropriate behaviour in a large department emporium, I quizzed Jill on this absence of class order and enquired whether they had achieved a truly egalitarian society. Jill said that in general poverty at the levels of my era had been eliminated, though the gap between the rich and those at the bottom had returned recently to levels last seen in the Victorian era and food kitchens were beginning to appear again. This suggested to me that a class structure still existed though not obviously apparent by the attire of the population on the street. Jill assured me that the English class system was still alive and well and although its application was possibly more subtle, she could tell a person's class by their deportment, confidence, manner and the attention to detail in their choice of clothing and accessories.

"These days it is not fashionable to flaunt one's class, Elizabeth, but everyone still knows their place."

Before I could find a way of asking, Jill said she thought she and James were somewhere between working class and lower middle class, though they did not in any way regard this as a stigma. I did not venture to put forward my class position as I felt they had formed an opinion already, which I hoped had not influenced our friendship.

"By the way, before you ask," she said, "you will find Jim to be what I call an armchair socialist steeped in Marx, Engels and the old Labour party. He does, however, restrict his politics to arguing with the telly and discussions down the pub where normally by 11 o'clock the world has been put to rights."

I made a mental note to look up Mr Engels' Condition of the English Working Class again for I didn't want to be seen lacking in this political arena, then I asked, "And what of the Whigs and Tories? Are they still at loggerheads?"

"Ha, well you won't believe this, but they've formed a coalition."

I didn't believe this and took this as sign that we should return to our reason for being in Chichester. I diverted our attention from the subject by pointing to a Farmers' Market in the centre and suggested to Jill we might find bargains there, but she said that they were actually more expensive than the shops. Then she took me by the arm. "Now, Elizabeth, enough of politics. Let us go and work our way down the most exclusive shops in North Street and if you find something to your liking which I think might be too expensive, just remind me of Loch Ness!"

---~---

J.

We returned at about tea time with a cartload of bags and an empty wallet and after tea I was 'treated' to what they called a floor show, where there was much discussion about tarts, frumps, what should be revealed, what should not and more importantly what needed to be taken back; which of course would mean another shopping trip and an attack on my wallet.

I must admit I found myself being a little bit more prudish than expected with Elizabeth's clothes, which was noticed by both of them and resulted in some banter at my expense from Jill, who suggested that my normal criteria of less is more was not being applied with my normal vigour. I also had the distinct impression that Elizabeth, despite the shock protests of the occasional slip in rearranging her new attire, was revealing as much as she intended.

Eventually we settled down, with Elizabeth choosing an outfit which a teacher at a nice school would find suitable. Her hair had been lightly cut to what the hairdresser had told her would be more 'manageable' with her curls loosened and now falling to her shoulders.

"So how did you get on at the hairdressers and more importantly how did you avoid talking about your holidays and your interesting background?"

"We decided I am from an old Anglo-Maltese family in Valletta on a long visit to England. I had visited Valetta as a child and therefore had some knowledge with which to converse. I also told her I had had my hair styled in an 1870s fashion specifically for a masked ball. This worked well and of course this allowed me to give great detail of my past without revealing my true nature."

I looked at Jill who said with mock surprise, "Aren't girls clever, Jim?"

I decided I'll never believe a word girls say again, especially if they are working in pairs.

Then I remembered Marco.

"Elizabeth, when did you last see Marco?"

"Why, driving off in a carriage from your cottage."

"So where is he now?"

"Or when" said Jill.

We decided to contact him in the morning.

---~---

Out of Time

$$\nabla \cdot D = \rho$$

$$\nabla \cdot B = 0$$

$$\nabla \times E = -\frac{\partial B}{\partial t}$$

$$\nabla \times H = J + \frac{\partial D}{\partial t}$$

Chapter Six

J.

The receptionist at Manchester said Marco had taken an extended holiday and was not expected back for a few weeks. Which meant he was either in Midhurst or was playing games in the 1870s.

Jill suggested we should visit the cricket clubs at Hamgreen or Midhurst to see if his whereabouts were known, but I was concerned that these could still exist as time portals.

"I'm a little afraid to do that at the moment, Jill. Marco said our time loops should be broken but these cricket clubs may still be sitting on nodes in space-time from which we could be transported inadvertently anywhere or any when. We could find ourselves in the distant past or future in a world which is far more hostile or unforgiving than now or in 1873. Marco also suggested that these time loops were being created and destroyed all the time. Whole new loops could be waiting for us only to break before we got back. In fact, thinking about it, Marco might even be stuck in 1873!"

"Then let's look him up to see if he's there."

"We already have," I said.

"Not in the 1870s. Remember, we looked up D'Ora. We didn't look under Marco Batalia."

We grabbed a tablet and started looking.

His name didn't appear anywhere in the 1870s but amazingly I did find an article on the Loch Ness monster.

"Hey Jill, we're famous. There's an article here about our Loch Ness monster in 1871. It was sighted by a Dr D. McKenzie, who described it as like an upturned boat which suddenly raced off at great speed. I think he was with Henry's shooting party."

"Any pictures?" She said with a look that indicated that my answer would greatly affect the length of my short life.

"No, don't worry, there are no photos or references to a mad semi-naked woman dancing on top of the monster."

I quickly turned to Elizabeth, conscious that I may have been a bit too vivid in my description, but was gratified to see she was having difficulty trying to hide a smile. She caught my look and then failed miserably to look shocked.

But then, while searching in 1873 for any unusual technological events, I came across Maxwell.

"Look! James Clerk Maxwell publishes his theory of electromagnetism in 1873!"

"So what does that mean?"

"Maxwell's Equations!"

"Jim, could you please elucidate a bit more for us mere mortals"

"Maxwell's equations combine electrical and magnetic fields and define the speed of light. They form the basis of all modern physics. We had spent hundreds of years trying to measure how fast light travels and Maxwell showed that it is an integral part of the fabric of the Universe. With no Maxwell equations, there is no Einstein, no General Relativity, no GPS, no space-time and more importantly, no Star Trek!"

Jill turned to Elizabeth. "As you can see, Elizabeth, living with a scientist …"

Elizabeth replied, "Dear Jill, try living with people who reject Mr Darwin with tedious quotes from every line in the Bible."

"Forgive me, Elizabeth, I didn't know in your time you knew we were descended from monkeys."

"Miss Urquhart, I do not believe we are not descended from monkeys. I believe that all species have evolved together and everything that lives today has found its own path and place here through natural selection and is not inferior or superior to us."

"So you don't believe in God?"

"Dear Jill, everyone, irrespective of their faith, will eventually find in some time of their lives the need to believe in God. Whether he exists or not, he will allow us to escape from the horrors of the reality that confronts us."

Jill and I looked at each other. "I think, Jim, that we must remember not to treat Victorian women with the contempt that some Women's Libbers think they deserve."

I had almost forgotten my train of thought. I made a quick mental note to remember that just because I lived a hundred years later than Elizabeth I had no claim to intellectual superiority.

I returned to the subject in hand. "Excuse me for digressing, ladies, but what I'm saying is: isn't it a bit of coincidence that Maxwell comes up with his theory in the same year that Marco, who says he is an astrophysicist and you agree has some considerable knowledge of space-time, turns up?"

"So are you saying, Jim, that Marco has gone back in time to help this Maxwell with his big sums so that time travel can exist so that Marco can go back in time to help Maxwell with … God, my head's just exploded again!"

"If I follow you correctly, James, we exist here because of Mr D'Ora and if we disturb him in anyway then, how can I put it, we would have never met!"

"I don't know, Elizabeth, but it is also possible he has other plans which we are not a part of. Thinking about it in hindsight, it is difficult to believe he just made the Loch Ness monster so we could be together."

"That means we could just be pawns in his game, James!"

"But this could of course all be speculation, Jim," said Jill.

"So do we do nothing and hope nothing changes, or do we

try to find out what he is doing and risk losing our existence?"

Elizabeth looked at me. "Do you think, James, if we return to our own times we will remember each other for if that is the case I confess I would be rather distraught."

"Unfortunately, Elizabeth, based on our experiences so far, we will remember everything."

"Then, James, whatever we decide to do we must do together so whatever happens we will still be together."

"That's very brave of you, Elizabeth, but I think we should wait until he comes back off his hols."

"Unless, of course, Jim, he's using his holidays as a cover for his plans." said Jill.

"Great, so do nothing or do something. We might as well just toss a coin."

Just then there was a knock at the door. We looked at each other.

"I'll get it. You stay here." And I went into the hall and opened the door.

"Hello Mr Urquhart."

"Marco!"

He was wearing the same collarless suit and zipped shirt he wore when we visited him in Manchester.

"Yes, may I come in?"

We all sat down. Elizabeth drew very close to me and held my hand, watching him warily while we all recounted at some length our tales and concerns.

When we had finished Marco sat back in the chair. "I see. Well, the truth is I can travel in time but I'm not the only one. There is another at Hamgreen Lodge."

"What, the chap who denied ever seeing Elizabeth and her sister?"

"Oh, you've been there. That makes it difficult."

"Why?"

"Because he's stolen my time machine."

"What! Why? How do you know it's there?"

"Because UPS sent me an acknowledgement of its receipt, one stasis box for the attention of Mr Batalia with the address. He obviously hadn't heard of postal tracking. The blighter even used my name and charged it to my account!"

"So", said Jill, "What's he trying to do?"

"He is trying to turn the world back to a more 'natural' state and remove all the scientific discoveries since around the time of Copernicus."

"What, he wants everyone to think the Sun still goes around the earth? Is he succeeding?"

"In some ways, yes. His first goal is to stop Maxwell publishing his paper. As you've deduced, if he removes Maxwell then there is no going back in time to stop him.

"So Maxwell knows what's happening?"

"Yes."

"And how is he going to stop Maxwell? If he bumps him off I'm sure some other bright minds will take his place."

"It's simple. He steals his papers and then works his way back through Newton to Copernicus. Imagine if you lost your university thesis and notes with no computer or cloud back up."

"God, you're right, it would be a disaster! But how do you know all this?"

"Because I found a diary of Maxwell's at Manchester, which describes a visit by a time-traveller who offered to buy all Maxwell's works in exchange for knowledge of a time transponder. Maxwell recorded that he smelled a rat and agreed to exchange the information but slipped him his 1860s paper on Physical Lines of Force rather than his equations. Before this chap had realised what he had done, Maxwell had gone public with his equations. But Maxwell knew that this chap might come back so he filled his diary with detailed information on time loops and nodes but more specifically the location of the nodes. He knew how to design a time machine but he also knew the technology in 1873 could not construct it."

"So you went back to visit Maxwell?"

"Yes, in fact I saw him several times. Told him about the diary and how I had constructed the time machine. He was most surprised to hear about it and claimed he hadn't written any such thing and certainly had not had any offer from any one to exchange his theories for a time machine."

"He must have written it after your visits, Marco," I said.

"Yes, that's what I thought. He was most interested in our world and especially pleased he was so famous and wanted to know everything about Einstein. He made me go into great detail about the past hundred years. I could see at times he was quite shocked by what had happened."

Elizabeth said. "I am not surprised, Mr D'Ora. I admit humanity is not perfect but now they seem to have the opportunity to be imperfect on a much grander scale."

I tried to put this together. "So he wrote out the instructions in a diary and lodged it in the University to wait for a time in the future when the technology and materials were available?"

"Precisely, and I constructed a machine and went back in time to tell Maxwell."

"So has this chap succeeded?"

"Obviously not yet, otherwise we wouldn't be having this conversation."

"My God! So we need to get over to Hamgreen Lodge and destroy your time machine!"

"Precisely."

"And how do we trust you?" said Jill, "You haven't been exactly straight with us on your previous visits."

"You can't, but I hope you can see that I needed to make sure your visits to the 1870s actually happened otherwise everything I'm trying to do might have changed. I can tell you one thing though: I don't want to live in an ideal world without our advances in science and medicine and … more importantly, I've got an incredibly expensive hole to fill in my bank account."

---~---

Out of Time

Chapter Seven

J.

We arrived at Hamgreen about eight o'clock in the evening. I parked the car on the main road away from the gravel drive.

"So, what's our cunning plan, Marco?"

"I'm afraid a bit of breaking and entry is required, but first we need to cut the power lines," said Marco.

"Sorry Marco but I didn't know we were auditioning for an action movie," said Jill.

"Perhaps, Marco," I said, "we should try and find the external fuse box to the house before we try to fry ourselves."

I suggested Jill and Elizabeth stayed in the car but Elizabeth was adamant she was going to stick to me like glue and Jill said she wasn't going to stay on her own another night, this time with only an ashtray for a bucket.

We approached the house through the wood to avoid the gravel. It was in darkness. Jill found the external white utility box, which of course required one of those special keys to open. I was disappointed to find that neither of the girls' handbags had one, but not as disappointed as they seemed to be in their expectations of me.

So I went for Plan B and broke the pane on the side entrance door, expecting burglar alarms and god knows what to go off. Silence. Then I reached for the handle inside, half-fearing that my hand would be bitten off by some rabid dog, only to find the door was already unlocked.

Jill whispered in my ear. "Jim, please tell me you checked the handle before you smashed the glass and woke the entire neighbourhood."

I looked to Elizabeth for support, who seemed inexplicably to be trying to hide a smile with her hand.

"Well we are in," salvaging my pride, "so let's go."

It was almost pitch black. I felt Elizabeth grasp my hand.

"Torch, Jim?"

I felt myself sliding further and further off my horse.

"Ok, ok," I said, "Plan C. Let's see if we can find a light switch."

"Shall we also put a big sign outside, Jim, saying, 'Caution: Amateur Burglar Training Night. Police Are On Their Way'?"

"Please Jill. It may have escaped your notice that this is not my day job."

"Really, so what do you do all day?"

I felt her overnight stay at Loch Ness was a memory that was going to take some time to fade.

"Look Jill, I'm doing my best, feeble as it is. Why don't you give our new 'friend' Marco some stick instead for not pulling his weight in the 'good ideas' department. Besides, if we can't find the light switch you know what that means?"

"No."

"It means we are in 1873."

This riposte gave me a little satisfaction for a moment, though luckily in the pitch black I could not see her reply. I found the switch. The hall light came on. It was 2015, thank God.

"Gosh James, it looks exactly like my house when I left it."

"So where do we go now, Marco? In fact, I'd appreciate it if you can give us a clue to what we are looking for before Elizabeth decides that …"

"It's easy," said Marco. "It's the box you were in, in Manchester."

We opened the hall door and I felt for the light switch on the wall behind, wondering why I still seemed to be nominated as Captain Intrepid.

The main reception room lit up.

"Hello Marco, hello Mr Urquhart, Miss Urquhart and this must be Miss Bicester. How confused you look, Miss Bicester. How are you finding being out of your time?"

His lack of sympathy in her plight roused my animal instinct. I stared at the man whom we had met at Hamgreen Lodge and who claimed he did not know us. I still remembered the look on Elizabeth's and Flory's faces. He sat in an old moth-eaten settee with a glass of red wine next to the stasis box.

"Maxwell!"

I turned to Marco, who had the shock of surprise on his face.

"Yes, Marco, and thank you for finding my diary and building the time machine."

Marco looked like he was going to sink into the ground.

"But where is the time traveller?"

"You're looking at him, Marco, oh, and thanks for the lift to your time."

"I didn't bring you back!"

"Oh, but you did. You just didn't look for me in the stasis box."

---~---

E.

I was quite shocked to see this person occupying my family house without any evidence for my or Flory's concern or wellbeing. I was determined to make my views plain.

"Mr Maxwell! Although I am pleased that I have met James and I have seen incredible things that most people would not be privileged to see, I am appalled that I have been used as a mere trifle in your scheme, literally ripped out of my time without askance just to satisfy your desires. And then you compound this with your audacity in asking how I feel! I assure you, Mr Maxwell, if that is your real name, if I had my hat pin you would feel the vehemence of my feelings towards you!"

I then turned to James for support who immediately impressed me with a vigorous defence, though I felt his language could have been somewhat tempered a little.

---~---

J.

I was just making a mental note to hide her hat pins when I realised that Elizabeth was expecting Captain Intrepid to do something and also to perform better than the last time we met Mr Maxwell. I had a lot of points to make up. It didn't take much incentive. I walk over to him and grabbed him by the throat and treated Elizabeth to what I presumed was some new vocabulary.

"Look. You've messed up this girl's life so you can return us to some crap ideal world where most kids die before the age of five and only stop dying 'cos their mothers have died in bloody childbirth. Believe me, I've seen the gravestones."

Maxwell yanked my hand free but stayed put in the chair. "Your world is unnatural, sir, and needs destroying. Mr Batalia has shown me what science has done to your world. Instead of a tool for advancement, it has become a tool for social engineering."

"Come on, the scientific method cannot predict or control human behaviour."

"No, but certain people have cleverly used science to develop highly technical communication systems which they use as conduits to control the masses. Everyone is now, as you say, 'wired in'. I think they are very close to making the human race unconscious!"

"Rubbish! And do you not think that we have the free will to decide how we live?"

"Look at your phone, Mr Urquhart, there is the clue in front of you. Do you carry it all the time? How many times do you look at it each day? Do you respond to every message? You are being conditioned, I say!"

I must admit he had a point as just then I heard a notification on my phone and it took some will power not to look at it. He noticed, however.

"You see how difficult it is to resist, sir? Your science is also destroying the material world, sir. In their quest to control human culture they ravage the precious minerals, rape the forests and pollute the atmosphere. It must be removed so that nature can take its natural course again and people are given back their free will! There is not much time. Look at the size of the world's population: it has increased almost seven times in the last hundred years. It has become a great hive created just to feed a few queen bees."

"That's not the fault of science! It's the fault of humans who won't stop breeding. Scientists made the Green Revolution to feed the world and the world bloody well carries on breeding at the same rate as it did in medieval times, except now the kids don't die because science has come up with ways to stop them dying! The only problem we have is to convince people they don't need ten blooming kids these days to ensure they've got a footprint in the gene pool!"

I was rather conscious now that I was ranting on a bit and was possibly as effective as when I shout at the telly during a party-political broadcast.

"Unfortunately, your argument is irrelevant because I have already succeeded, Mr Urquhart. I have destroyed my electromagnetic thesis and now I will go back to 1873 and not publish them. Then I will use this machine to visit Newton and his Royal Society friends and remove their papers. Then the means by which the world is controlled will cease to exist!"

I was beginning to feel I was in the presence of some Wellsian master of the universe.

Then, just as I reached out to grab him again I saw Marco run past me to the time machine.

"Yes, Maxwell, but unfortunately for you your equations are so famous that most physics grads can derive them from memory without even trying. All I've got to do is go back to 1873, write them up and publish them in your name in London. Hold him, Mr Urquhart!"

And with that he rushed to the stasis box. Just before he closed the door he turned to Elizabeth and held out his hand. "Last chance, Miss Bicester?"

I looked at Elizabeth. She was looking at the portal. And then she stepped forward. I felt myself falling through the floor. Around me time stood still.

She came towards me looking straight into my eyes, and said, "Goodbye Mr D'Ora. I will take my chances here."

"Then goodbye, Miss Bicester." And Marco turned and entered the portal and in a blink of an eye disappeared.

Maxwell groaned with despair.

---~---

E.

We left Maxwell in his chair. I imagined him now trapped in James' world with nowhere to go. I almost felt sorry for him. As we walked down the drive to James' carriage I thought I could hear him screaming.

We slowly drove back to James's cottage. I thought about Mr D'Ora and his machine and where he would go, and what powers he controlled. I wondered whether any human being could remain benevolent with such a tool. Then I noticed James was silent. I feared I had made a dreadful mistake.

"James".

"Yes Elizabeth, I'm sorry for my language but I ..."

"No, James, I understand but I - I fear I have made an awful imposition. I did not ask you if I could stay."

He turned. His shoulders relaxed.

"And Elizabeth, when Marco asked you to join him I realised almost too late that I had not asked you stay with me. Please forgive me?"

At this point Jill, who had been staring out of the window, turned towards us and quite shocked me in her suggestion, for which much later I came to thank her.

"Look will you two just get out of the car and go in that field over there and don't come back until you both realise, what is patently obvious to anyone else, that you love each other."

---~---

Comment by Professor Rolleston

Both diaries end here, which made it difficult to believe that they were not contrived, though it was possible a significant event involving both the diarist caused the entries to cease.

Never-the-less, I thought it the end of the matter and returned to my normal researches.

Then one morning I received a disturbing communication from the Weber Institute informing me that the diary purported to be written by James Maxwell had been discovered in a house in Midhurst.

Apparently, the diary contained his mathematical formulae on the electrical and magnetic properties of light and its application to space and time. There was also described within, instructions on the building of a machine which could move within these dimensions.

The Institute felt that in view of the possibility that such a machine, if constructed, could alter the fabric of time and cause changes to reality that would be detrimental to the ComsMesh social structure, I was required to return to the Institute immediately and recommence my studies of the diaries to ascertain what I could gleam from their contents on time travel.

When I arrived there, I found a note and flat black plate on my desk about half the size of a foolscap with a green flashing light.

I picked up the note. It read simply;

> *'The withholding of any information regarding the whereabouts of Mr James Urquhart or Elizabeth Bicester will result in excommunication from the Institute.*
> *Dr M. Batalia, Director of SocAction, ComsMesh.'*

As I had withheld nothing from the Institute I did not understand this threat. But as I pondered its implication my eye caught the green flashing light.

I turned to the plate and noticed below the light were the words 'press here'. My curiosity led to me to obey its request and to my amazement the plate dissolved into a white page which contained an extract from Urquhart and Bicester's diaries!

I picked up the plate and as I did so new pages appeared! I quickly discovered by pressing parts of the plate that I could move back and forth through the diaries and I immediately turned the pages to find the end but discovered instead there were recorded dozens of new diary entries!

I sat down in disbelief for I realised that far from completing my work it had only just begun.

I began immediately. But the task was far from easy as the texts did not always appear in chronological order. Worse, I later found that the couple seem to occupy many time lines and it was with extreme difficulty that I managed to assemble their recordings into some semblance of sense.

However, eventually I managed to make sense of some of it and located the pages which I thought continued from where the two physical diaries finished.

As you will see from my following narrative, it was not long before I realised the ominous note accompanying it was addressed to me.

--~--

Part II Down the Rabbit Hole

Chapter Eight

E.

I had not been in James' attic before and I allowed him to climb the ladder first.

A yellow glow suffused a panelled room illuminating five of those dark mirrors which I had seen everywhere allowing entry to other people's lives. He pressed a lever and a Mercator map of the world appeared on one mirror on which, by means of typewritten instructions, he overlaid a net of the red, green and blue lines which I understand to represent the distribution of the electric telegraphic cables and connections between towns and cities. I could see they concentrated on the great cities of the empire but also the Americas and China. He then illuminated a second dark mirror which displayed a blue green rotating globe which I quickly recognised as our world, though by what means this vision from space was contrived was beyond me.

As I watched fascinated I felt myself begin to fall towards it until I realised it was the effect of magnification. In a moment England filled the mirror. Then, by further instructions, he first displayed the electrical cables by which his world was powered then superimposed the electric telegraphic net.

"Look, a node in West Sussex," he said. "I'll magnify it."

I felt myself falling again at an impossible speed towards Sussex.

"James! Slow down, you are making me giddy! But wait, look at those lines converging on Midhurst. Can we go closer?"

James moved a lever and I could see that the lines converged near the ruins of the old Cowdray House. By further magnification the ruins of old Cowdray House filled the view.

"Gosh, this must have been a beautiful place before it was ruined. It's either Elizabethan or Jacobean. Do you know its history?"

"I know the house was burnt down. My grandmother remembered the great fire. She said there was a great curse on the family. Apparently one of the ancestors removed relics from Battle Abbey and a monk cursed him saying, 'Your line will end in fire and water.'

"And only 200 years later it burnt down. And what about the water? Did the owner drown in a fire bucket or too much water in his gin?"

I reminded him that in his illuminated cocooned world, ghouls, ghosts and phantoms may seem to be entertainment for children's minds but in my world of flickering candles, rattling window panes and black nights only occasionally illuminated by a flickering moon, the 'other' world was much closer.

"Yes, you're right, Elizabeth. I remember we were in bed in an old house in Norfolk where because of the antics of a single rat we were quite willing to believe the 'other' world and all its creatures were waiting for us outside."

"James, you might think curses are old-fashioned, but the Viscount died on the Rhine Falls two weeks later and his sister's two sons were drowned in the sea near Aldwick."

"My god! I can see how that curse became famous. I must pay more attention to my grandma."

"Yes, James. By the way, you said we - was it you and Jill in the bed?"

"What! Oh er, No! ... Ah, another world. Look, Elizabeth, the lines don't intersect on the house but between the bend on the River Rother and that old church. I'll get a map."

Although he changed the subject quickly, I was gratified that he looked suitably embarrassed. He opened the map.

"See here," he said. "It's an old Norman castle just on the bend of the Rother. The lines intersect here."

I looked up to him and he misinterpreted my regard as an inquisition. He took my hand.

"I have a past, Elizabeth."

I took a great risk. I looked him in the eye and reaching for his hand and holding it tightly I said, "And so do I, James."

His smile and kiss lifted a great burden from me.

"Now," he said, returning quickly and cautiously to the matter in hand, for I had no wish at this stage to indulge in the subject. "What do you know about the castle, Elizabeth?"

I tried to remember what my governess had told me during our history lessons. "I think they were built after the conquest, like Chichester, Arundel and Bamber."

"I'll look it up. No, nothing. But wait a sec. Look who lived in Midhurst! H.G. Wells. That's too much of a coincidence."

"I do not know him."

"Oh, he's very famous. Let's have a look. Ah! He's after your time. He was only seven years old when I met you."

"What is he famous for?"

"He wrote a story about a man who invented a time machine."

---∼---

J.

By independent enquiry we had arrived back at Marco. I had seen at Manchester his time machine and the amount of equipment needed to power it and that led me to the conclusion that a vast amount of power was required. I thought if I looked at a map of the power distribution and the comms network I would be able to trace its origin. There were many nodes around the country but I did not expect to see one in Midhurst, a place not normally known as a hotbed of advanced science and engineering.

The icing on the cake was, however, H.G. Wells and his Time Machine. He must have met Marco or collaborated with him. What was interesting was whether his fictional story was actually a record of some of Marco's exploits. Then I thought about his other science-fiction novels. His history of the future, The Shape of Things to Come. Was this the real future or just one of many? As for his War of the Worlds ...

We had been staying in Chichester since Elizabeth's arrival and spent much time trying to impart as much knowledge as possible on the last hundred years. With regard to her ability to absorb information Elizabeth was full of surprises. Yesterday she had asked me if I could explain Maxwell's equations to her. As their derivation usually required both my neurons I did not expect it to go well. However, when I showed her the equations she became very excited and was soon extracting and writing down everything I knew on tensors and field equations. In her best copperplate they looked like a work of art. Apparently, I discovered, Elizabeth was quite good at maths and had spent the previous year at Girton College studying part of the new Mathematical Trypos. Jokes about Girton girls and the difficulties in climbing the guardian walls or getting passed the porters were, however, not well received and I was reminded I should concentrate on how difficult it had been for a girl to get a man's education rather than their availability for recreation. Although I noticed an enquiry about 'recreation' caused an immediate change in topic and suggested someone liked to 'party'.

Unfortunately, any further conversation on that topic was stopped by her placing Einstein's deceptively simple equation in front of me and asking me to explain and derive each term.

We got to bed quite late. The intense concentration of a Victorian's brain, devoid of the distractions of TV and media sites, was quite exhausting.

---∼---

E.

He was very kind and considerate in his explanations of the field equations which required understanding a significant amount of new algebraic notations. I hope he did not regard me as too much of a dunce and if I ever meet my tutor Miss Emily Davies again I hope she would be proud of me. I think I may have complained too much about how my writing had suffered with his automatic pens for he has found and given me a 'fountain pen'; it has improved my copperplate significantly though I must remember not to keep reaching for a non-existent ink pot while I am writing.

But I must return to the subject. The nexus of electricity and telegraphy over the castle must indicate the presence of Marco's time engine or at least its origin. I asked him for his opinion to which he replied.

"Well, there's only one way to find out."

---∼---

Out of Time

Chapter Nine

J.

What was left of the castle, which apparently stood on a mound called St Ann's Hill, were various courses of wall about half a meter high covered in ancient oak trees and scrub. We found no recent excavations or evidence of secret tunnels. However, I had no doubt there was something underneath because a little app on my phone which measured crude magnetic variations showed significant anomalies as we traversed the centre of the Hill.

We went back into Midhurst and decided to look for H.G. Wells' house. It was situated in North Street and for confirmation there was one of those blue plaques recording his digs there. We also found the old chemistry shop on Church Hill.

By now it was getting late in the day and we agreed that we should stay overnight in Midhurst so we could spend the following day exploring. There was an old coaching inn opposite the church and we decided to book in there. I asked Elizabeth if she wanted a separate room, but she said she would rather have her honour compromised then be left alone in a world she barely knew. And besides no one here knew of her reputation. I didn't argue.

Our room was very olde-worlde. Typical tourist's four-poster, sofa and an old telly on top of a brown chest of drawers. The leaded glass windows looked out to the church across the road. There were two internal doors. One led to the ensuite bathroom. The other was a part of the original building, very narrow and only about 5ft high. It seemed locked but after giving the handle a good hefty twist I got it open. There was a waft of damp air. I opened it further and to my surprise I saw a stone passage.

"Elizabeth, come here. Look what I've found."

"Gosh, do you think it is a priest's hole? I believe the early dukes were staunch defenders of the Catholic Church and at one point there were dozens of what were called recusants living in Midhurst."

"Recusants?"

"Catholics, James. You know, people who were not Anglican like the Dukes of Norfolk at Arundel, or have you forgotten how religious our country has been? Even in my mother's time there were still restrictions placed on Catholics. By the way, do you have a religion?"

I thought it best not to be flippant with someone who possibly had gone to church every Sunday all her life.

"My father's family were Scottish Presbyterians and socialists and I was christened in an Anglican church, which I believe my grandfather regarded as a papist. So the best I can say, Elizabeth, on the subject of religious belief is that I am very confused."

"You have my sympathy. I have friends who through love have married Catholics and it caused no end of family squabbles. Anyway, what shall we do with this passage? I presume from my past experience with you we are about to explore it."

Not wishing to disappoint Elizabeth by having my unasked-for accolade of Captain Intrepid questioned, we descended the steps using an LED torch I kept in the car and my phone compass. I was hoping to record the route, for no other reason than if we got lost, but my phone's GPS was useless. The walls were lined with rough local sandstone bricks. There was green moss on parts of the passage, indicating that it had been illuminated. After about ten metres it turned right, which

I surmised was in the direction of the church. The passage floor had human track marks indicating perhaps recent use. After about fifty metres there was a passage on the left. We followed it until we reached a nailed door. It was locked but I could just see through the key latch what looked like the church crypt. We went back down to the passage and continued. After a while I could hear a faint hum. Suddenly I noticed a light on the ceiling connected by wire to a switch on the wall. I tried the switch and a row of lamps lit up the passage in front of us, at the end of which was a door. I turned off the lamps and continued cautiously. I held Elizabeth's hand tightly, hoping she would think it was for her support and not mine. Another ten metres and we arrived at a steel door. I decided to push it and to my surprise it opened easily.

---~---

E.

This was the first time I had travelled with him on my own.

After many trials I had selected clothing which conformed to his world's fashion but gave me some pretence of modesty. Jill had tried to persuade me to wear trousers, but I felt that they gave away too much of my shape and left virtually nothing for the imagination. Jill, I was pleased to say, agreed and said that a good figure and close-fitting trousers did draw frequent though sometimes unwarranted attention and had the disadvantage of reminding one of failed promises to undertake a regime. I had not reached this conclusion yet as I was still enjoying the liberation from the corset and dare I say by my observation of many modern ladies I had some way to go before I need worry about refusing the offer of cake.

After exploring the castle ruins and the old town of Midhurst James reserved a room at the coaching inn at Midhurst. The proprietor had done his best to preserve its character in a way in which someone of James' era would regard as Victorian. He had persuaded me that we should reserve only one room for the night and I was surprised how little persuasion I needed, though I insisted that I must pretend we were married to preserve some semblance of a reputation, and so I saw for the first time my name recorded as Elizabeth Urquhart.

The passage that we had discovered led us to a metalled door which James easily opened, to reveal a hewn cavern. In the centre stood a large plinth surrounded by electric contraptions with large dials and levers. Rows of little green and red lights winked on and off on black and gold metallic boxes attached by hundreds of electrical cables. Across one wall I noticed there were clocks, dials and levers connected by brass and copper pipes and in the centre of the room a large rotating globe of our world with dials showing what looked like dates and times.

In a corner an elderly gentleman stood over a desk regarding a black mirror intently.

---∼---

J.

I recognised H.G. Wells from his photographs as I walked slowly towards him. He turned and before he could speak I said, "Hello, Mr Wells. What year is it?"

He looked at us with less surprise than I expected.

"1895 sir, but I can tell by your clothing you are from the future, though your companion has the air of someone closer to my time."

There was only one question I could ask of H. G. Wells.

"So you do have a time machine?"

"No, I do not have such a machine, but I am acquainted with someone who does. And who, sir, are you?"

"I'm James Urquhart and this is my wife, Elizabeth. We're looking for a Mr Batalia who had a time machine."

Elizabeth turned to me but said nothing and gripped my hand more tightly.

"And newly married it seems, or maybe incognito?"

Before I could reply he continued, "Mr Batalia has disappeared and so has his machine, but before he left he told me what he had seen. It was very interesting. In fact, so interesting that I have recorded and published his story as a fictional novel."

I knew which of his novels this was.

"And what he told you, do you believe him?"

"He said he had a contraption for travelling through time which he would demonstrate to me if I was interested."

"How?"

"He appeared at the chemist's shop where work in town and asked me if I would like to see something that would be of great interest to me and my future. I must confess I was attracted to his proposition as I felt I was at an impasse in my life. He brought me here and showed me his contraption and told me of his time travels. Then he entered his machine and disappeared."

"Did he mention anything about us?"

"No, he did not sir. Why, what interest do you have in him?"

I stalled as I needed to understand why he was here.

"He brought my wife and me together. But why did you think it was a time machine? It could have been a conjuring trick."

"Before he went I asked him if I could publish his memoirs in the form of a novel. He agreed, then went to a desk and retrieved a plain package which he gave to me on the condition I should not open it until I had published. I agreed. I returned here today after visiting my publisher Mr Heineman in London and opened the package."

He showed me the contents. As I had already guessed it was his Time Machine novel.

---〜---

E.

I was a little shocked when James announced we were married but I understood his motive a little too late.

I suggested in a whisper to him, but with some humour I might add, for I did not want to pre-empt a possible event to my liking, that in my time it was taken as good manners to ask a lady first and wait until a satisfactory reply was received before announcing they were married. In fact, even a wedding ceremony was regarded in some circles as a prerequisite.

He replied in the same humour that he was profusely sorry but he thought it would preserve my honour and if the occasion to propose ever arose he would go down on one knee and ask for my hand in the most traditional way. To which I drew attention to the fact that up to that point I had not realised my honour was in question. Feeling one of his innuendos on honour and marriage coming on I pressed my finger gently to his lips.

However, I could also see that Mr Wells was more concerned about his discovery of time travel than our relationship. James pursued with further questions.

"Mr Wells, do you know where Mr Maxwell is?"

"Mr Batalia wanted to meet him. Why, have you met him, Mr Urquhart?"

"I last saw him at Hamgreen but that was in my time."

"Mr Batalia was very concerned about Mr Maxwell, for he believes he holds the key to time travel. Do you know how the time machine works?"

"I've used it, Mr Wells, but I'm more interested to know

why you are here."

He looked at us a little sheepishly, like a child who had been caught in the cake tin.

"My curiosity got the better of me. I wanted to see if I could time travel myself, but I am at a loss with these computational machines."

Then James said, "Perhaps we can help. Do you know what these dials and levels do?"

"I believe they control the travelling of the vehicle through time. See these dials, I think they show dates. I think they are the chronological locations of the vehicles. I have discovered that by manipulating these levers and slides the dates can be changed. Watch."

He lifted a lever and began to slide a knob along a slot. The year on one of the dials changed from 1895 to 1874.

"Then by manipulating this Vernier I can home in on a particular date in the year." On adjacent three dials the month, date and hour moved to 3rd of April 1874.

"So, these dials could show the year and day where the time vehicle could be," I said.

"Or," he said, "one is for the time vehicle, another for this chamber and the third is for the world above us. Did you see any dials like this on the time machine, Mr Wells?"

"No Mr Urquhart, which suggests the travel was set from here."

An idea came to me. "So James, what would happen if we changed them all to your time?"

They both looked at me, then we both looked at Mr Wells who, taking on board my suggestion, proceeded to move the dials to 2015. At first nothing happened. Then the air above the plinth began to shimmer and within another moment a black capsule materialised.

"It's the box Marco had at Manchester!" said James.

He went over to it and pressed a button and a door slid open.

We entered. It was empty. Then we left quickly for we realised we had left Mr Wells in charge of the dials.

"You know what this means?" I said, suddenly realising what we had done.

"Yes, it means Marco is now stranded in some point in time without the means of getting back. Can anyone remember what the dates were set at? And more importantly, which dial does what?"

---~---

J.

We moved the first dial to 1900. Nothing happened. We moved the second dial and the time machine disappeared. The third dial did nothing.

We moved the second and third back to the present and the machine reappeared. I then went back down the passage to the pub. When I got to the door of the White Room I opened it and found a rather dirty room with candles and a moth-eaten bed. The first dial obviously moved us backwards and forwards in time which meant the whole chamber under the castle was a time machine as well. I wondered how much power our actions had consumed and more importantly whether anyone had noticed.

When I got back to the cavern I set the first one back to the present and returned to the pub. I was in the present time again. Then I repeated the process with the third dial and the time machine disappeared. I went back up the passage and found nothing changed outside.

At this point Elizabeth, who I thought had just been patiently wondering what I was doing, said, "James, change the hour on the third dial again. Look at the globe. There is a pointer over England."

I looked at the slowly rotating earth. A brass point hovered over southern England. I turned the hour hand clockwise and the pointer moved east.

"It's showing right ascension that means there must be ... yes, here it is. The declination dial numbered 0-90 degrees."

I turned the hand and the pointer moved towards the north.

"It's a spatial locator. This dial sets the location of the time machine."

"Which means we can go anywhere in space and time. I could go back home!"

She saw my look and once again held my hand. "Not without you. Now what are we going to do with this contraption?"

"Well, we have Marco running loose and Maxwell brooding at your house. I think we should go and see Maxwell to listen to his version of events again but we must not tell him we have a time machine yet. For all I know he's been here. Are you coming with us, Mr Wells?"

"No, I am going into Midhurst in my time but first I will set us to your time so you can safely get out."

"Actually", I said, "we'll set it to your time and you can leave first."

Wells looked at us, shrugged his shoulders, and then agreed. Once he had gone we set it to our time. Just before we left Elizabeth said, "What is to prevent him coming back and using the time machine to contact Mr Batalia?"

This was a good point. I looked at the machinery. "You're right, Elizabeth. We need to immobilise it."

I looked at three dials and their associated levers. I tried to open the dial glass but they were sealed. However, the brass handles on all three associated levers were unscrewable and I removed them.

"This may do it, Elizabeth. But for all I know these handles just appear again in different times."

We returned up the passage to tour room in the pub. It was our time.

We decided to book a week at the Coaching Inn to make sure we kept the room to ourselves and then drove down to Hamgreen.

Maxwell was waiting at the door.

"So you have come back. I am in some way pleased because I am stranded out of my time. What do you want?"

"We need to know what you think Marco is doing."

"When he first visited me he came in his time machine and told me I had invented it. I denied this but he then described to me how one might travel in time. He said that if I didn't invent it then his time machine would not exist."

Elizabeth said "This suggests, that there are parallel worlds or multiple universes"

"It is more like at each point along our time line there are multiple or random choices at the Plank level."

They both looked at me then Elizabeth said, "So why at each point do we not go off in different directions in time. What I mean is why we are all still here together?"

"There are infinite choices. So there's at least one universe where we all stay together."

"I think, James, you may be on the edge of your comprehension."

She was right of course. On the molecular level, following my suggestion, at each infinitesimal point in time our atoms should be going off in different directions.

I proposed that we must all be locked in one timeline, but each point depended on events in the past and a change of any historic event would change the future. Elizabeth, who I was beginning to think could give Einstein a hard time in a debate, said, "Do you mean our lives are already mapped out for us?"

"No, well, I hope not. I think we are free agents and the future depends on our past. Thus if you change the past you change the future."

"And" said Elizabeth, "you can only change the future if you have a time machine."

We both looked at Maxwell. He looked like the chap who invented dynamite for the purpose of quarrying and found that it became remembered as the explosive weapon of choice for war.

"So, Mr Urquhart, Marco is trapped in 1873 with all my research notes."

"Yes, but he hasn't got the technology or power supplies to construct a time machine to get back."

"Unless Wells has sent the machine back to him," said Elizabeth.

"God, I'm an idiot. They could be working together! I hope those handles will stop him."

---~---

E.

To see my home again gave me mixed emotions. I knew I was out of my time, but I hoped that somehow Flory could be there to meet me.

I needed to be home. My bed, my favourite chair, the comfort of the soft candle light and the smell of an apple wood fire in the hearth with James. With James? I realised I wanted him with me in my time. Perhaps all of us just want to go home. But I knew now was not the time. It was occupied by Mr Maxwell and now James had proposed Mr Wells was working with Mr Batalia we may have lost our only chance of going back.

While contemplating my changed life suddenly the air in front of me shimmered and momentarily distorted and the time machine appeared. The door slowly opened. James moved close to me. Out stepped Mr Wells.

"Well, that worked. Thank you for your help Mr Urquhart. Now ..."

Maxwell rushed for the door of the machine, but James stopped him just in time. "And where are you going, Maxwell?"

"I am going home to tear up my papers."

"Well, I'm afraid Mr Maxwell you cannot because it is only set to go from here to Midhurst," said Wells.

James, who looked very perplexed, said, "How did you use the machine, Mr Wells? I removed the control handles."

"Oh, it was easy. I just put my penknife in the slots and manipulated the sliders to the right position."

James had that look he had when he broke into my house and felt he had not quite measured up to my expectations.

"OK, now that we are all together," said James, "I suggest we all go back to the control room in the time machine and discuss our plans there. We can't manipulate time here."

"Just a minute Mr Urquhart," said Mr Wells. "I've come here post-haste because when I returned to my world, Mr Batalia was sitting in the public bar of the coaching inn."

"What, you met Marco!"

"Yes, Mr Urquhart, I went up to him to thank him for his memoirs on his time machine as it had been accepted for publication and I had received a very generous fee of £100. He was studiously writing and when he turned he was quite shocked to see me. He then blustered a little and wishing me well hastily gathered up his paper and after a quick adieu he left."

"So, Mr Wells, what was so important?"

"Well Mrs Urquhart, in his haste he left this." He removed from his waistcoat a folded piece of paper which he handed to James.

It was a letter to a Professor Rolleston warning him on no account to discuss Maxwell's diary and to report to Dr Batalia immediately if he had any information on the whereabouts of James Urquhart or Elizabeth Bicester, otherwise he would be excommunicated from COMSMESH. I grabbed James' arm.

"James! We are fugitives. What have we done?"

"It seems we've learnt more about time travel than is good for us, Elizabeth, and the clue is in this name ComsMesh. Mr Maxwell, do you know where your diary is?"

"Yes, it is lodged in ..."

James stopped him in his tracks. "Stop, don't tell me. The less people know the better."

Then James whispered to me, "There may be bugs in here."

I shivered and quickly looked around the room. "How big are they, James? Do they fly?" For I am quite nervous of spiders and daddy-long-legs.

"No, Elizabeth. I mean listening devices or even cameras watching us. We must get inside the machine. Humour me for a moment and pretend you are going to faint. It is important."

I was much relieved though I could see James wasn't. I played his game.

"Oh James, I am going to faint. I fear this conversation on time travel is too overbearing for me and now I am a fugitive from I don't know what!" And I collapsed into his arms which I must admit took him quite by surprise.

"Help me, gentlemen, my wife needs some air. Help me to the time machine."

And we went inside with James carrying me in quite a close fashion which I could tell he was enjoying at my expense.

James turned to Maxwell. "She has left her handbag on the

sofa with her smelling salts. Quick Maxwell, get them before she faints again."

Maxwell rushed out and James closed the door behind him. I was already holding my bag.

"Now, Mr Wells, get us back to Midhurst quickly!"

Wells started the machine and in seconds we were back in Midhurst. I gently released his grip and gave him a demure look that told him I was aware of his actions, then played that I was much relieved and felt better.

"Thank you, Elizabeth. It was the best I could think of to make sure Maxwell didn't come with us."

"And why don't you want Maxwell with us?"

"Because he and Marco are trying to change time and I don't know why. We need to find out what ComsMesh is."

---∼---

J.

When we got back to the Midhurst cavern, I could see Wells was quite concerned. I decided to tell him our whole story with Marco, how Elizabeth and I met and the time travels. He was extremely interested and said it had all the makings of a good novel with the right pen and embellishments. I was rapidly coming to the conclusion that Mr Wells' only interest in life was writing adventures.

"Well, Mr Urquhart, I think there is still much to be found. I almost wish my friend Mr Conan Doyle's Sherlock Holmes were here to help. I think I need to go back to my own time and retrieve my notes of Mr Batalia's memoirs for there may be something in them which could be of use."

I wasn't too happy about him leaving but as we seemed to have control of time I agreed it would be a good idea, and if he could find out where Marco was living that would be useful as well.

After he had left we set the outside world back to our time.

I needed to make the time machine inoperable. Mr Wells turning up at Hamgreen was quite a shock.

"Elizabeth, we really have to find a way to stop people using this infernal machine. There must be something in here we can remove."

We went inside. There were only two or three controls and the camera. Where was the power supply? I tried removing the levers but to no avail. I then tried to remove the console panel by loosening the screws with a coin. It came off to reveal a block of three fuses. I took a quick breath, hoping to not to get electrocuted, and pulled them out. The faint hum I could hear in the cabin died. We then went back along the passage to our room in the pub.

On arrival I got out my laptop and we searched through the internet looking for ComsMesh. At first, I could not find anything although a number of sites came up with a media company called Adcom. I tried a couple of the sites and they seemed to be just one of the hundreds of little web companies trying to compete with Amazon or Facebook. I then found on about the twentieth page of Google a PDF page and opened it. It was a correspondence on file sharing, peer-to-peer systems and privacy. Halfway down it mentioned a conduit called ComsMesh. Nothing else. I looked up Adcom, which seemed to occupy the first ten pages on Google. It had over a hundred million subscribers! It had a simple business plan. They offer stuff they think you want and if you buy something at least once a month you can keep your subscription. I wondered which of the big media companies owned it but to my complete surprise Adcom actually owned three of them including two of the big social networks.

I decided to go on to the Adcom site and subscribe to see how it worked. I picked up an email address and a fictitious name, Andrew Dent, and put them in. The reply made me almost jump out my skin.

"Hello, Mr Urquhart. Thank you for joining us. We have linked all your social messages in one place for your own convenience. Please choose as an introductory offer one of our free gifts."

"My god, Elizabeth, they know who I am and everything about me!"

Not only did they know my name but I saw my lists of messages not only from my various social media clubs but from my emails as well. They had every electronic communication!

"Gosh, James, you have a lot of correspondence and hundreds of photographs. May I see?" And she gave a rather mischievous look that suggested she knew what she might find.

"Perhaps, but only if you allow me to read the diaries of your teenage years."

"Ah, touché, James. You would know all about me and a lady could never allow that."

"Yes, our pasts do make us what we are today, but they are not necessarily what we are now. Anyway, let's see if I can get out of this."

I tried to unsubscribe.

"To unsubscribe, Mr Urquhart, please follow the instructions below. Please note in unsubscribing all your media messages will be deleted."

By one simple action I had locked myself electronically into Adcom. No wonder they had so many subscribers.

I checked the legal stuff and newspapers. Apparently by subscribing all my messages became the property of Adcom, although I was free to keep printed copies or download them for personal use. This also applied to all those media companies I had previously subscribed to that Adcom had bought.

---~---

E.

I could not imagine all my private correspondences with my friends and acquaintances on public view. What would one become in society? A slip of a pen or private judgement and a person could be ruined. I mentioned this to James, who said this happens all the time and often leads to break-ups of friendship or vitriolic attacks on one's character. I decided this was not a medium for me and also if I ever returned to my own home I would burn all my diaries from my younger years, for I would not want James to discover them and make judgements on my infatuations.

James had by a simple action now unfortunately surrendered all his personal correspondence to a company who I imagine could do with them what they wished. I pointed this out to him.

"James, this is terrible! This electrical medium in which you correspond. What is to prevent them altering the content? They could turn you into a criminal or make you say things about your friends which were not true! You would have no redress."

I could see he was mortified by this.

"God, Elizabeth, what we have done? You're right. We have handed over our past to alter as they will. They would have the power to control the world. They could destroy political opposition at a stroke! I now see what Maxwell was trying to say. Marco had described this world to him and he'd seen what could happen."

"And he blamed himself and thought if he could destroy his discoveries, Marco's world would not exist"

"Well, Elizabeth, the good news seems to be that Marco is the villain, not Maxwell. And the bad news is we have to go back to see Maxwell, who we have abandoned twice now."

I could see there was merit in what he suggested. Mr Maxwell was the key to Mr Batalia, but I was getting very tired and did not feel up to another challenge at that time.

"But it is getting very late now. Perhaps it would be better to go in the morning?"

"Good idea. Now let's sort out sleeping arrangements."

I had almost forgotten about that in the excitement of what I can only describe as the day's adventure. I had to remember that what I desired and what was protocol were two different things. I was gratified that James helped me out in more ways than one.

"Elizabeth, I'll sleep on the sofa with a couple of your blankets and you in the bed. I'll pop down to the bar for a couple of drinks while you get ready."

I did not want him to leave. "No, I do not want to be left on my own next to that time tunnel. Anybody could come out."

"How about I wait in the bathroom until you're ready. I promise not to peek," he said with a grin.

"And how am I going to do my ablutions?" I must confess I was enjoying testing him.

"Oh dear. Right, you get abluted and I'll wait here. When you're ready I'll face the wall and will definitely promise not to peek. I'll cover my eyes. You could even blindfold me."

I was beginning to feel we were acting like two silly children trying to be good in front of their parents.

"Alright James, you do not have to blindfold yourself but I don't want to catch you turning around," I said with a smile. "Though I am sure you will try."

I managed to get into bed without too much difficulty

though I could not help but smile at him, who was doing his utmost to face the wall without looking around. However, just as I was pulling up the sheet to make myself look as 'respectable' as possible in our situation I noticed the mirror and realised he had cleverly or should I say deviously stationed himself against part of the wall which afforded a perfect view of me crossing the room and getting into bed!

I must confess I could not blame a man who has affection for a lady wanting to view her dressed in her private garments – less especially as this particular lady had willingly allowed herself to be alone with a man of her affections in a bed chamber! I was now, how can I say, in a delicate position which depended a lot on his response. I decided to play him at his own game, hoping his humour would suffice for I did not want to lose this match. I played my first card.

"James." I said with the most seductive voice I could muster.

"Yes, Elizabeth?"

"You can turn around now."

He turned and looked straight into my eyes. I could feel him pushing open a door. I played on.

"By the way James, that sofa does not look very comfortable. Are you sure you will be able to sleep there? I would not like you to catch a chill," I tried to look as demure as possible.

"I'm sure I'll be alright."

He played his card well.

"Perhaps I could help." I said.

He looked as expectantly as I hoped and then I played what I hoped was my trump card, or as it recently had become fashionable to call it, rather aptly, the Joker.

"Could you turn that mirror to the wall for I feel it is reflecting too much light in your direction?"

It was at this point I wished I had his 'phone for it would have made a perfect picture to treasure.

"I'm sorry, Elizabeth. I just couldn't resist it once I noticed it was there. Please forgive me. I'm having great difficulty with, how do you say, courting a Victorian lady who I love. I get so confused with protocols and manners and what will not offend her."

I held my last card for only a moment then put it before him.

"I know, James. Now come to bed."

---~---

Out of Time

Chapter Ten

J.

We woke rather late and had a nice leisurely breakfast in the inn. For some reason I was in no hurry to leave. In fact, all I wanted to do was just drive off to some quiet little cottage and live with her forever.

Elizabeth seemed equally content.

---∼---

E.

There is something about a shared intimacy which dissolves the gap between time and space. That morning at breakfast I noticed he had for the first time relaxed considerably in my presence and was fussing over me, making sure I had everything I wanted. I let him and found myself thanking him profusely on each suggestion. I was surprised how easily I surrendered to him. It was so nice to be 'looked after', if I may permit myself to try to imitate one of James's innuendos. I had not realised, and this is difficult to write, how much of my intimate self could respond to such physical pleasure.

We left the inn about 10 o'clock and travelled back to Hamgreen again. Mr Maxwell was still there. He took a little persuading to allow us entrance.

"So you agree with me that your world is being manipulated, or are you just worried about your own safety?"

James said, "Both, Mr Maxwell. But I do not think the solution is to remove your equations. Up until thirty years ago society was not wired in, and I feel that is the point where we must cause a deviation to prevent social media expanding. Before that it was just the role of journalists, advertising and politicians to manipulate us. But then we let everyone join in."

"In that case we must find out where their operational base is, for knowledge of that will give us an indication of where to start."

"I'm not convinced they have one. They could easily be individuals working together in the dark net - unaware of each other but sharing a common purpose."

Just then I remembered the letter Mr Wells had showed us.

"James! Did not Mr Wells' letter refer to a Professor Rolleston? Perhaps he is the key."

He immediately took out his phone and entered instructions to locate him.

"No one obvious."

Then I remembered the date on the letter.

"James, what year are we in?"

"2015, I hope. Why?"

"Because there was a number on the letter at the bottom, 2021. I did not think more about it until now. The number must refer to the year the letter was written. When Mr Batalia met Mr Wells he must have come back from the future! Which means if we want to contact Professor Rolleston we must travel to the future as well."

"Elizabeth, just in case I forget for some reason, will you remind me to marry you at the earliest possible opportunity?"

With the same humour I said I would do my best to remember.

"OK then," James said, "If we contact Rolleston we had better return to Midhurst and set the time to 2021. Coming, Maxwell?"

"Undoubtedly, Sir. And if there is opportunity to get out of this time it would be most welcome".

We returned all three of us to the Cavern and adjusted the time controls to 2021 and James tried his phone again

"I'm in luck – I'm still with same service provider. Ah! Here he is. He's working in the Department of Social and Cultural Engineering for the Weber Institute. Now where do they hang out?"

James searched again. This amazing device for instant knowledge was a marvel. I could see why it would become quickly indispensable. I made a mental note to ask James how I could acquire one.

"Ah. They hide in Chichester just behind the University. Let's give them a bell and ask for him. I'll put it on speaker phone so we can all hear."

He telephoned. After a minute a curt voice spoke.

"Rolleston here."

"Hello, Professor Rolleston. James Urquhart here. I believe someone is looking for me."

There was an audible sharp intake of breath. James tried again.

"We're looking for Mr Batalia."

"Mr Urquhart, I do not know where he is."

"Good, but we do. He's trapped in the past around 1895 and we have his time machine."

"You have the time machine? What do you want?"

He sounded very worried.

---~---

J.

I seemed to have Mr Rolleston in a corner, though after my brass handle and broken window affairs I did not hold much hope.

"The first thing we want to know is what you want of us."

"I'm not at liberty to divulge that."

"OK, that's up to you. While you're thinking about your liberty we will go back to the 1870s, destroy Maxwell's papers and then destroy the time machine. Oh, and also your control centre. Any problem with that?"

"But you can't! Society would collapse. We are close to bringing together a system that will save the world from destruction."

"I think the only thing you're close to is your plan for world control."

"We have discovered the means to socially engineer populations. We can remove much of the randomness that causes waste and war."

Maxwell interjected. "And in doing so, Mr Rolleston, you will remove the human will and its inventiveness, sir. Do you think I and my colleagues would have been allowed to make our discoveries on the nature of electromagnetic radiation? I think not. You will put boundaries on our quest for knowledge and then you will slowly constrict it until we are all in stasis. How will you deal with new natural catastrophes or diseases?"

There was silence. I continued.

"So, Mr Rolleston, I'm beginning to understand how all this time travel came about at last. You discovered Maxwell's diaries, which showed how to make a time machine."

"Actually, we found your diaries first, Mr Urquhart."

"What?"

"Yes, yours and Miss Bicester's. Found in a box in Hamgreen Lodge. I wrote a thesis on it trying to prove that they recorded real events and therefore time travel existed. I'm glad to say I've been proved right."

I looked at Elizabeth and she looked at me. "You've kept a diary too, James?"

"I've kept notes of everything that has happened in the hope of it all making sense, and I still have them. What about you?"

"Why, I still have mine. So why are these diaries at my home?"

I began to understand what was going on. Marco mentioned it when he said he was in a time loop at Loch Ness. Time travel had not only caused a corporeal shift but also affected the mind.

"I think this all starts with us. At some point in the future we will return to Hamgreen and put our diaries of our adventures together."

I decided to test Rolleston.

"Where were they found, Mr Rolleston, and what did they look like?"

"In the attic, clasped together in a metal box. Miss Bicester had a leather-bound book and yours was a thick black note book."

Elizabeth and I looked at each other in surprise. They were our books. But I also now knew where we should put them if, if what? ... I decided to press on.

"So Professor, let's get back to Maxwell's diaries. I bet they contain a conversation between Marco and Maxwell. So you knew you had to build the machine so that Marco could go back to Maxwell and help him formulate the functions to build it. But in doing so Marco revealed to Maxwell the world order you were creating. Maxwell was not happy. His papers were already published so he needed your time machine to go back and destroy his papers and those of the people who contributed to his theory so your world would not exist. Is that not right, Mr Maxwell?"

"That is right, sir. I gave Mr Batalia the wrong papers in the hope that he could not progress and so would return instead, which he did, unobserved by me. While he looked for my papers I boarded and hid in his time machine. He brought me to Hamgreen where I later met you and Miss Bicester. I found out where he was working and the location of the time machine and had it transferred here. I used his computer at

Hamgreen to access his bank accounts."

"But why Hamgreen, Mr Maxwell, and not Manchester or his Control Centre at Midhurst? What was he doing at Hamgreen?"

Rolleston interjected, "To see if he could find more information about your diaries."

"No, Mr Rolleston. I mean, how did he know they were there?"

"Miss Bicester's father had advertised an auction at the house. I have an interest in old books. The diaries were for sale, so I bought them. I could not make sense of them. They looked like notes for a novel but their dates were separated by over a hundred years. I sent them to a colleague to date them who confirmed the dates were correct. That was when I began to suspect time travel. When I found that H.G. Wells had published his time machine novel shortly after Miss Bicester's diary I became almost certain and flagged it up to my directors."

Why was there an auction? Was the house up for sale? Elizabeth and I looked at each other. Where or when did this all start? What was the initial cause? Was it a time aberration with Marco at Midhurst transferring him to the cricket match in 1870? Or when I walked onto the game at Hamgreen in 1873 and met Elizabeth. If there had been no time aberration then Adcom and ComsMesh would have achieved their goal without any trouble. Did this mean that these time warps we were participating in had been created somehow to stop ComsMesh?

I suddenly had a thought. Where were all the servers storing ComsMesh's data? The amount of power needed ... It had to be in the cavern at Midhurst. Had the immense power concentrated in such a small place caused the initial time shift that rippled through the years, sweeping up me and Marco? I had certainly picked up strong magnetic signals on the castle ruins with my phone. I tried to imagined distortions in time and space appearing around the servers at Midhurst and coalescing into nodes as the time dimensions struggled to find paths of least resistance. Perhaps when we entered and used those nodes they became stronger, forming a new or parallel time direction which we were now in. The problem was, how stable was this timeline? I needed to get back to 2015 quickly, in case the timeline disappeared. I turned the dial and cut off Rolleston. I realised I still had no idea how the time-travel machinery worked.

---∼---

E.

I was still shocked that we had sold or would sell my home. Even more concerning was that it was my home in the first place as I was sure that in my time a lady could not own or inherit property. As my father had only daughters I expected the house to be transferred on his death to his nearest male relative, my cousin Henry. This I must admit was of no great concern because my cousin, when I had broached the subject, told me that we would be allowed to live at the lodge.

I pointed this out to James who was really surprised that women did not have these rights and "looked it up" on his phone.

"Ah Elizabeth, it seems you can inherit. A law was passed in 1872 giving women the right."

"So it seems that I will inherit our home. But I still do not understand why it would be sold."

I then noticed that Mr Maxwell was studiously looking at the controls, and so did James.

"What are you doing, Maxwell?"

"I am trying to figure out how this works and I am led to

the conclusion that it is not a time machine, it is a machine for manipulating a point in time."

"Do you mean a time node?" said James.

"Yes, that is a good word and I think that Mr Batalia's time machine is a container in which he has trapped one of these nodes, which he can manipulate from here."

So," I said, "if I understand you correctly, if we release this node or knot of time from his box, time travel will no longer be possible?"

"Except," said James, "at the moment in the future they have Maxwell's diaries, so they could start all over again. What is really scary though is that everything we're doing now they may know about. In fact they may actually be watching us!"

I hoped that they had not been watching everything that we had been doing. Then I tried to sum up.

"So, we have Mr Rolleston in the future with our diaries, Mr Batalia trapped in the past. Mr Maxwell from the past with us now and Mr Maxwell's diaries in the future."

"And Mr Wells wandering in the past looking for Mr Batalia." James added.

I began to feel we were running around in circles.

"So what are we trying to do? I mean where do we want all this to end? As far as I can see we could just walk out and leave everything to carry on without any harm to us."

"Except, Elizabeth, in this timeline we become wanted persons and we need to find out why. We need Marco."

We both looked at James.

"Look, I'm not spending my life wondering when the Time Police or whatever they call themselves come to get us. At the same time we can't destroy the time machine because Rolleston and ComsMesh will just carry on. Somehow we have to get Marco to do it."

"But first we need some clothes for the period," I said,

"Otherwise I will be taken for a woman who escaped from a mad house or even worse, one of ill repute.

---~---

Out of Time

Chapter Eleven

E.

James took me into Chichester where he found what he called a novelty shop hiring out period fashions. Actually, it reminded me of one of those occasional shops in Brighton where ladies who had 'accidently' exceeded their allowance and were reticent to ask their fathers or husbands for additional funds could temporarily lodge garments in exchange for a small pittance to avoid embarrassment. We eventually hired some clothes despite my protestations that I would look like they had been borrowed from my mother's wardrobe. I told him that I hoped I would not meet any of my acquaintances for I was sure I and these garments would become a topic of conversation at my expense for many years to come in certain circles. I was reminded of my grandfather who despite our insistence that he should change his fashion would invariably arrive at engagements in garish hose and breeches.

James in his hacking jacket did not fare better and looked exceedingly like an American card sharp rather than an English gentleman, but at least I had dissuaded him from his first choice of a 'festive' and rather 'sudden' striped jacket with matching cap.

We returned to the cavern, changed our clothing and turned the time back to 1895. Then, summing up courage for our reception, we returned to the passage and my world. We thought it best to come out in the crypt of the church just in case our room in the inn was occupied. We tried the door latch, which had been locked in James' time, and were gratified to find it opened. We went through the church quietly past two old parishioners in the pews who tried not to notice us but gave the distinct impression that their topic of conversation would be us for the rest of the day.

We arrived at the coaching inn across the road from the church and went in. James was already a little unnerved as he had seemed to attract more than his fair share of local dogs as he crossed the road, which he cheekily attributed to the fact that they were not used to the odour of someone who washed twice a day. I responded that a lady might prefer a gentleman who washed less but at least had money to pay for meal and lodgings. He immediately produced his wallet and removed some notes so as to show me that he had sufficient funds. However, when I suggested that the coinage of Queen Elizabeth would not be as well respected as Queen Victoria's in my time he looked a little crestfallen. This was not helped by the attention he continued to receive from a small Irish terrier which had attached its molars to his trouser leg. Poor James was then reduced to asking if it would be alright to borrow some money. I thought it prudent at this point not to remind James that it was impolite to ask money from a lady.

By chance both Mr Maxwell and I had a little money. I gave mine to James, who protested at first but agreed once I reminded him that in my time a lady seen paying for a gentleman in an inn would have provoked considerable comment against her reputation and dare I say much speculation regarding her occupation.

We booked two rooms with James and I taking one and Mr Maxwell the other. The landlord seemed a little perplexed by our dress but happy with the colour of our money. He also, I think, believed I was James' wife. Then to my horror I noticed one of Henry's friends sitting in a corner playing cards! He noticed me but I think he did not recognise me as my hair was different and my clothes were not of fashion. Nevertheless, I resolved to draw no attention, put my arm in James' and went up to our chamber, hoping not to meet any other acquaintances coming down.

James examined closely the bed and covers. "Well, at least it's clean and it looks like they've washed the sheets since the last occupants."

He then looked for what he described as an ensuite bathroom and was rather disappointed to find only a linen cupboard. A discussion on the methods of ablution and toiletries I am afraid led to further disappointment and a rather uncalled for comment about our needing a good 'scrubbing' when we got back to his time.

As I regarded the chamber I felt a yearning to be back in the nice clean and neat chamber of James' time. After readjusting ourselves in front of a worn mirror and helping James with his tie, we went back down and dined with Mr Maxwell. I was pleased to see Henry's friend had left.

We had just finished, and James was trying to persuade me that he should have another jug of what he described as their excellent beer when Mr Wells came through the door. He recognised us immediately.

James apologised to him for not offering to buy him dinner as he was, as he put it, 'a bit short', carefully omitting, I noticed, that he was 'a bit short' of my money. To our surprise Mr Wells produced a five-pound note and gave it to James, saying that he had been paid handsomely for his novel and was sure that our 'adventure' would provide another novel for which he expected a similar recompense. James immediately found use for it by buying another round of the landlord's 'excellent' beer.

On finishing his meal Mr Wells recounted his story.

"I met Mr Batalia. He was very upset being trapped here with no communication. He had been to the cavern and found the brass handles had been removed. He, like I, tried to use a penknife to operate the machine but, to my surprise and his, it would not work."

"That's because," said James, looking much relieved, "we found a better way to immobilise the time machine."

"Well, Mr Urquhart, I don't know how you did it but he is definitely trapped here."

"So where is he now?"

"I do not know at present, but I do know he will be at the cricket club in the morning, for there is a game against the Fotheringale Eleven. Have you heard of them?"

I felt the ground falling away and steadied myself against James.

"It is my cousin's team. Most of them will know me! I dare not think what would become of me if I am seen!"

"Well, I'm afraid we have to meet him there. If we leave it any longer he may find a way to operate the time machine," said James.

--- ~ ---

J.

The next morning we walked up to the cricket club. We spotted Marco straight away. He was in his cricket gear and polishing his bat. I quietly walked up behind him, watching the bat closely and said, "Hi Marco. Want to go home? "

He nearly jumped out of his skin. "You! What have you done to the time capsule?"

"I've disabled it. Why, is that a problem?"

He stood up holding his bat in the same fashion as when I had first met Elizabeth's cousin. For some reason I continued.

"You must be running out of money. I expect you've noticed the old social welfare net isn't too good here."

He came towards me but then he saw Elizabeth, Wells and

Maxwell, and thankfully relaxed his grip on the bat a little.

"What are you all doing here?"

"You left a letter, Marco. A letter to a Professor Rolleston indicating that Elizabeth and I were causing a problem. Do you remember?"

"So that's where it went. Still, I cannot see how it is any use to you."

"Except Marco, you mentioned ComsMesh, which then led us to Adcom. I subscribed and they took all my emails and media stuff. We know what you and the Weber Institute are doing."

I could see that our discovery of the letter and the function of ComsMesh was a complete shock to him.

"So now you know, but what can you do about it? You can't change the future."

"Are you sure? How many futures are there? Perhaps we can't change this future but perhaps we can change to another future. One without time travel."

"What makes you think you can do that?"

"Because Mr Wells believes the novels he has written are a record of the future. But it is not mine, Marco. That tells me different timelines can exist."

He could see what I meant. "What are you going to do?"

"It's simple, Marco. If you destroy your servers, wipe everyone's personal data and close down ComsMesh you can go home."

"You destroy the servers and no one goes home."

"Ah so the servers are an integral part of the time travel mechanism. That could explain a lot. So how about we do it in my time, Marco, rather than now?"

I looked at Elizabeth, who nodded vigorously in agreement and at the same time was looking anxiously around the club for any sign of her cousin's cricket team.

"Do you know what will happen if the servers are destroyed, Mr Urquhart?"

"Yes Marco, you will lose all your subscribers and their personal data. There will be some disruption but everyone will think it's the result of some massive cyber-attack."

He looked at me, carefully weighing up what I had said and then to my surprise he said, "You will first have to catch me."

And he ran over to a horse tethered by the fence, leapt on and as he rode off shouted back, "And I will be back to the time machine before you, and you will be trapped here forever!"

I really hoped the fuses in my pocket would stop him.

I turned to the others.

"We must follow him"

But Elizabeth had a look of shock on her face. I turned in the direction of its cause and saw her Cousin Henry coming towards us.

--- ~ ---

E.

To my horror Henry had recognised me. He was walking towards me. I could think of no defence and I was sure even James would be tested beyond his powers of persuasion. Then I noticed he was smiling!

'Hello, Elizabeth, I am glad to see you again and looking so well."

He turned to James. "And if I remember correctly this is the gentleman you ran off with. Are you looking after my cousin, sir?"

I was not quite sure what he meant by that phrase but James immediately adopted the tone of the conversation with equal politeness, though I am sure he must have wished to be any when but there.

"Thank you for your enquiry, sir. I am sure if you are acquainted with your cousin Elizabeth as well as I am you will know that she is very capable of looking after herself, to which I might add I regard her with great respect."

"I am pleased to hear it, sir. Her mother always regarded her as a bit of a handful and if she has respect for you, sir, then that says much about your character."

This conversation about my character in my presence was a little trying to say the least and it was compounded by the fact that I realised that any interjection by myself would only reinforce their assessment of me. More so, I do believe they were aware of this and continued in this vein for over a minute at my expense! I can only say that none of it was too derogatory.

Henry turned to me.

", Elizabeth, I have never heard you so quiet. Have you lost your tongue?"

I found that I had. Then he took both my hands and said, "Are you happy?"

"Oh Henry, you have me cornered. I am very happy and to reply to your first question," I looked at James, "I am 'looked after' very well but I must tell you we are in a great adventure which may alter time itself and are very pressed."

"And Mr Urquhart, is he from a different time?"

At first I thought I had misheard him but his expression indicated he had some understanding.

"Yes, Henry."

"And do you know, Mr Urquhart, what will become of me?"

"No, sir. In fact I do not know what will become of us but I assure you whatever happens we will be together."

Henry nodded and turned back to me. "I just want you to know that we will look after your house for you if you ever come back." And with that he kissed me lightly on the cheek, shook hands with James and returned to the club house.

We were now much behind. We walked and ran as fast as we could back to the church and the passage.

--- ~ ---

J.

When we arrived back at the cavern I was much relieved to find Mr Batalia was still there. He had the console lids off. I showed him the fuses. "Are you looking for these, Marco?"

He made a rush for me and was stopped in his tracks by Wells, who had produced a pistol! I looked at Wells and then the gun.

"I am in a real adventure, Mr Urquhart, with things I do not understand, dangerous things. I felt a pistol may be needed."

I hoped the gun stayed pointed at Marco. I continued. "Marco, I want you to get in the time machine. I'm going to let you go to the time of your choice."

He looked at me, Wells and the gun. "Now in you go, Marco. What year would you like?"

He was confused, then his confidence returned and he said, "Well, as I have little choice I would like to go to 2015."

I could see what he was trying to do. "OK Marco, 2015 it is then. In you get."

He got into the machine and closed the door.

I put the fuses back quickly. I heard a reassuring hum and then reinserted the brass knobs.

"What year shall we choose for Marco, Elizabeth?"

"How about the year after, 2016, then he can't interfere."

"Good choice."

I turned the dials and with a shimmer the time machine disappeared. "So Mr Maxwell, what years would you like?"

"To where I began, Mr Urquhart. If I understand your plan

there will be no need for me to destroy my papers."

I set the cavern to the time of his choice and he left via the passage. Then I turned to Wells.

"Mr Urquhart, this has been a great adventure. As you know I have seen some of the future with Mr Batalia and as a consequence I have recorded what I have heard and seen. I have here my notes on two novels I will write. There is already interest in the publishers of the Pall Mall Magazine."

He reached into his coat pocket and produced a thick wad of paper. There were two titles, 'The War in the Air' and 'The Shape of Things to Come'.

"I am not convinced it is a good idea to know the future, but they may help you, Mr Urquhart, when you return to your own time."

I took them gratefully imagining how much Wells' original notes for those books would fetch, then suddenly I realised what he meant.

"Mr Wells, have you heard anything about an invasion from Mars?"

Elizabeth looked at me incredulously. "An invasion, James? From another world?"

"Yes, it's one of Mr Wells' most famous books." I turned to Wells.

"Yes, Mr Urquhart, Mr Batalia told me it occurs in your time and takes place in the south of England. You will see that although I do not mention the narrator's name, both he and his wife survive."

His look gave no doubt as to who the two persons were.

"Now Mr Urquhart, can you send me back to 1895? I have work to do but before I leave I wonder if I could borrow your diaries. As we now know, Professor Rolleston found them in a box in the attic at Hamgreen which at the moment is impossible as you still have them."

Elizabeth and I looked at each other rather sheepishly. He continued. "I understand your reticence but if they are not put there this convoluted timeline we are following will not exist, or at least part of it may not."

"So, to ensure everything that has happened so far, we have to give you our diaries so that Rolleston can find them."

"That is correct, Mr Urquhart, so I will put them in a box in the attic in your home at Hamgreen Lodge where I think they will be safe until he can retrieve them."

"And if we don't agree?"

"Then it is highly probable that you two never meet."

"And how do we trust you to do this? For all we know you may have your own agenda or you're in league with ComsMesh."

"All I can say, Mr Urquhart, is that if I don't do this then none of my novels will exist. I will not become famous nor, more importantly, rich. And quite possibly I will spend my life in a chemist's shop. To answer your question, I do have an agenda."

"It seems, James, that once again what we decide greatly affects the future."

"Well Elizabeth, I've decided."

"And so have I, James."

I pulled out my notebook and gave it to him. Then Elizabeth removed from her bag an exquisite leather book held shut with a small clasp and gave it to Wells. He looked at them and then retrieved a small bound tablet from another inside pocket. He seemed to have a lot of pockets.

"Thank you. I understand this is very hard for you so I am giving you in their place the narrative written by Professor Rolleston which combines both your diaries."

I took the tablet and opened it. A white screen appeared on which I saw a recording of our first meeting at Hamgreen.

Elizabeth looked over my shoulder.

"Gosh, James, so that's what you wrote on our first encounter. I see you noticed me straight away and oh, you thought Flory and I looked like models from a Tissot painting!"

"Yes Elizabeth, and here is your description of me!"

We skimmed through the pages. Whoever had collated our diaries seemed, I must admit, to have captured our characters and humour rather well. I turned to the last page in the narrative. It was yesterday! I looked at Wells. He knew what I was thinking.

"I understand that your diaries are connected somehow to this device. As you make records in your own diaries it also records them as a narrative based on your characters it has gleaned from your writings. I believe from what Mr Batalia told me, if you continue to write up your private diaries the contents will be transposed to this device. It is beyond my comprehension. My only conclusion is it can read your thoughts!"

"And who else can read our thoughts, Mr Wells?"

"As far as I know sir, it is only between you and this contraption."

I wondered how many of these contraptions there were listening in to us. The sooner the time machines were destroyed the better.

I gave the tablet to Elizabeth. "I think it's best if you have this, Elizabeth. I wouldn't be able to resist looking at your private life."

"Thank you, Jame but you do know I will not be able to resist reading yours."

"All I can say is if we continue to write our own secret diaries we'll know each other very well."

"Yes, and dare I say too well. We are not a species that has advanced sufficiently to cope with unrestricted telepathy. If we regard a diary as a receptacle for our innermost feelings, this device will betray us!"

I agreed. I wondered whether we should keep it, then decided it might be safer in our hands rather than others. I turned to Wells, who understood.

"I fear it may be like a Pandora's Box, Mr Urquhart, to be kept closed and opened at one's peril. You must do with it what you will but personally I would destroy it as soon as possible."

"The problem is it might be tied up with our time path. We need to think about this and make sure we understand what the consequences of interfering with it are."

"Well, I have had enough of adventures and I would like to go home. I have a lot of writing to do."

We thanked him for all his help and set the machine to his date. With a farewell he left. Then I set the cavern to 2015 and turned my attention to the servers.

"I'm going to try and stop the servers, but it will mean we will be stuck in my time. Are you sure you are ready?"

"James, I made that decision when I came to your house in Chichester."

There were four monitors displaying data load and capacity bars. The red portion of the bars indicated they were still only about 30% full. Marco had plenty of space on his servers.

I pressed one of the green red bars and a warning line appeared at 50% and action limit line at 80% appeared at the end of the bar. They were touch screens! I had an idea. I pushed the action limit line slowly down the bar until it went into the red part. As I expected, a red warning sign started flashing on the screen. But then the red bar slowly moved back until it reached the limit line and then the other server red bars started to increase. The red warning symbol vanished.

"Look, I've reduced the capacity of one server and the system transferred it to another. I wonder what happens if I moved the limit to zero?"

"I'm afraid, James. I am really outside my sphere of knowledge. You must follow your instinct."

I moved it. The red line moved back to zero then the other red bars increased from 30% to 50%. They were taking up the load capacity!

"What does this mean, James?"

"It means, I hope, that these lines determine how much information can be stored on each server and also the transfer rate."

"So, if you move these lines along to the beginning of the bars they will not be able to hold any information."

I looked at her, amazed at her instant comprehension.

"Elizabeth, as well as being fluent in Latin and devouring Maxwell's equations, are you sure you don't have a degree in computer science as well?"

"It is just simple logic. I see no application of computational skills at all. I know in my time the application of logic was not expected of a lady and it required considerable skill on a lady's part to ensure that her nearest and dearest came to a logical conclusion first but I thought I would not have to exercise those skills with you, James."

"Elizabeth, I'm afraid to have to disappoint you, but even in my time an intelligent girl, if I ever came across one of course," enjoying her expression of mock horror, "is expected in public to pretend that her husband is generally in charge even if it is obvious to him and everyone else he is not."

I could tell she enjoyed that. The constraints on her in her own time amongst men of lesser intelligence must have been very trying, though I did feel at times she was making up for lost time at my expense.

I then returned to the subject in hand, wondering why I was so easily diverted by Elizabeth.

As fast as I could I pushed the lines on all the bars back to zero at the same time, wondering why I had not come to this idea considerably earlier and hoping that was not going to be Elizabeth's next question.

To my relief the red bars on the other screens started increasing and orange and red warning signs appeared. I rushed to the other screens and repeated the process. Orange and red warning signs started flashing on all the screens. I could hear mini alarms activating on the consoles. There was a noticeable reduction in background hum. The servers were shutting down! I imagined the panic at the Weber Institute. All those Adcom subscribers were now unable to access their accounts and there was no way the billions of people and their data could be reconstructed. The hum died down. The servers with no data had shut down. It was finished. Poor Marco would arrive a year too late in a time machine that was useless.

---~---

E.

I was touched that James had offered me the diary, especially as I knew he was aware that it would be almost impossible for a lady not to 'accidently' glance over a gentleman's diary. However, when I mentioned this later he told me not to worry as he wasn't a gentleman and therefore there would be nothing of interest for a lady. I almost fell for his bluff. Nevertheless, I hoped his notes, if I were to 'accidently' regard them, would not change my opinion of him. I also told myself that he would expect to read mine, though as a gentleman, which he is! I knew he would never ask.

When I do have the nerve to offer mine to him to read I

must resist scoring out any comments in my diary that might be to my disadvantage. Truth is everything in love.

James' suggestion on how to destroy the machine was marvellous. I was surprised that he had not thought of it before, though I did not mention this as hindsight is a wonderful thing especially if it is simply explained, which James is very good at doing.

After the machinery had become silent we retraced our steps to the coaching inn. Our room was as we left it though I did notice it had been tidied in our absence and the bed made. No doubt servants had different names now.

I desperately needed a change of clothing and badgered James, who had just settled down to what he called a well-deserved jug of beer, to take us back to Chichester.

We were greeted by Jill, who immediately took sympathy with my plight and whisked me upstairs. When I came back downstairs he was sound asleep on the sofa. I decided not to disturb him and instead went into the dining room with his sister to recount our tales and adventures. Jill, however, was much more interested in our relationship and managed to corner me into a confession which I was pleased to note was well received though her directness was difficult to parry.

After a while he awoke and joined us. He looked agitated.

"Have you seen the news? An organisation called the Dictatorship of the Air has just decreed that it is to make all religions illegal, and the air police have been sent to Mecca to close it down."

Jill looked at him. "So what's the problem? They've been preparing that for ages. What's wrong?"

"Oh my god, we are in Wells' timeline. We have taken a different path!"

I did not understand at first, so I went to the black mirror in the other room. It was showing a new motion image, a town. People were running down the street. In the distance I could see what seemed to be gigantic tripods from which beams of horrific light dissolved buildings in its path. Across the bottom of the mirror words rolled from right to left. I ran back to the other room.

"James! Martians have landed at Woking!"

---∼---

A Letter from Mr Wells

Before continuing with my narration of how the diarist dealt with the Martians, I feel it is important to present a note I received from Mr Wells on the placing of the original diaries at Hamgreen. His involvement in the matter of their existence is still not clear but I feel he plays an integral part. I also suspect he has an ability to travel or manipulate time lines for he often appears at critical points in the diaries. But for what purpose, I am unsure.

Dear Mr Rolleston,

In the course of my meetings with Mr Batalia I had the opportunity to read a copy of your narrative of the Urquhart and Bicester diaries. Mr Batalia informed me that the world in which we stood depended greatly on the retrieval of the original two diaries and their placement in a specific location in Hamgreen Lodge. In effect, without them my novels would not exist.

The narrative in his possession was recorded on a covered black rectangular box about quarter of the size of a foolscap paper. Opening the cover revealed an illuminated sepia screen containing a page of typed text entitled 'The Urquhart and Bicester Diaries'.

There seemed to be only one page, but Mr Batalia showed me by pressing either side of the screen further pages of text could be revealed. A small dot in the top right-hand corner of the screen glowed intermittently between amber and green. Mr Batalia explained that the device was connected to the diaries of Miss Bicester and Mr Urquhart and through an algorithm devised by ComsMesh.

Based on the narrative and knowledge provided by Mr Batalia, I was able to deduce that at some time Mr Urquhart and Miss Bicester would eventually want to meet with Mr Batalia again and would discover the time control centre at Midhurst. I then resolved to visit the chamber each day after work in the hope of meeting them. In addition, I also asked the local innkeepers and hoteliers to inform me if an unusual couple arrived for lodging. After several weeks a maid from the Spread Eagle informed me that a couple had arrived who were strangely dressed and asked for lodgings. I immediately went to the cavern via the church crypt. There I was fortunate enough to meet them and strike up an acquaintance which eventually allowed me to obtain their diaries.

My difficulty was placing the diaries in Hamgreen Lodge. However, I ascertained from Miss Bicester's diary that her sister should be living there and that if I told her the truth of their adventures she would be willing to look after the diaries for me.

On arrival at the lodge I was relieved to find that I was very much welcomed by Flory Bicester when she heard I had news about her sister and implored me to tell her everything. I then showed her the diaries and explained as well as I could that everything that I told her depended on the diaries being found in her attic by yourself. She took this very well, especially when I told her that the act would result in a very high probability of not seeing her sister again.

H. G. Wells

Part III The Martians

Out of Time

Prologue

E.

It was disease that ended the war as Mr Wells had said. Luckily, we had stayed with Jill at the cottage in Chichester where we were protected from much of trouble though all day and night for weeks I witnessed the machinery of war pass through and over the town. The armies of James' world were terrible to behold but I was thankful they were there. Long lines of great armoured carriages and cannons painted in all the colours of the earth rolled by and overhead black whirling machines and sleek silver birds like winged harpies flew in flocks darting and diving overhead. Their noise was deafening. Occasionally out of sight or sound from behind the clouds, rockets would rain down and later the muffled sound of enormous explosions could be heard beyond the Downs. At night the northern skies lit up with hellish fireworks and flames. Green and red lanterns rose and drifted along the hills illuminating them with ghoulish colours; lines of light traced out where mortal conflict ensued. And then the reality of it all would be brought home by the screams of sirens heralding the return of those who had been wounded or injured. I was amazed to see how different soldiers had become. Gone were the red tunics and the smart lines of a regiment on the march. These soldiers walked warily in groups like skirmishers at the front of a line battalion encased in what I can only say was mediaeval armour and carrying rifles with the power of a regiment in my time. Their clothes were so baggy and camouflaged they would have turned a poacher green with envy. These armies could have blown away our empire in a flash. We also watched on the dark mirrors the tide of battle which slowly seeped our way from afar - until Mother Nature came to lend a hand.

The time machine and the world of ComsMesh had vanished as had Mr Batalia. But there was one thing that remained. The electric diary that Mr Wells had given us. Each day as I wrote in my diary this mysterious contraption continued to record James' and my thoughts.

One felt that there was someone watching, somewhere in time.

---~---

J.

She had coped very well. To be taken out of her time and confronted with a war with aliens. Much of the world and its infrastructure had survived and I had been able to use the confusion of the war to get Elizabeth a range of immunisations without too much questioning. She had more importantly been given an identity tag by the military which circumvented a lot of questioning on her origin and allowed her access to a range of help, not least of which was food.

That was three months ago.

The staff of Porton Down were still trying to cope with their popularity after having spent most of their lives being vilified by the public.

The time diary continued to record our thoughts. Why had Wells given it to us? I agreed with Elizabeth. Someone was watching. We needed to understand what this device was and why it was created. Also, why had we ended up in Wells' time line?

I had managed to wire up a connection to my computer. However, the operating system could not be accessed nor could I open the case or understand how it was powered.

There was no reset button. I suspected its control was elsewhere.

---~---

Out of Time

Chapter Twelve

E.

There was much language and mutterings which I would not expect to be said in front of a lady coming from the attic. Nevertheless I decided to enquire and found as I expected James hunched over a desk surrounded by wires and notes addressing the electric diary in a way that was unlikely to acquire voluntary cooperation. He sensed my presence. He had gone to great lengths to find perfumes and eau de cologne which reminded him of our first kiss and although I was much attracted to more modern perfumes I respected his indulgence.

"God, Elizabeth, this is doing my bloody head in!"

"So I heard, James, and I seem to have acquired a number of new words and phrases which I had not realised were related to that electric diary."

"Oh, I hadn't noticed the door was open. But this thing ... What's making it work?"

He was sitting in an extraordinary chair which swivelled in all directions and looked as though it had the comfort of those found in a gentlemen's club. He had told me it was a great aid for thinking, though on occasion I had found him thinking so deeply that it was virtually impossible to rouse him from his thoughts. Suggestions that he was sleeping was always met by vigorous though eventually humorous denial.

On one occasion I had found him engaged in a fantastic war against almost impossible odds in which by means of a dark mirror and a small stick attached by a cable he was able to defend himself against hordes of soldiers. My concern for his safety not to mention his incredible courage in defending us was unfortunately dissipated when he explained it was just a "game" and demonstrated this by repeating his battle before my eyes. I think it was some modern equivalent of young boys playing with tin soldiers though why James was playing with such things at his age I do not know. Perhaps this is what men need. In truth I was much gratified that his participation in 'battle' was only make believe for I had known not a few war widows from the disasters in the Crimea.

He put his arm around me and drew me close.

"Look at this screen, Elizabeth. There's a slight pulsation in the brightness but that's all. It just sits there almost winking at me."

He turned to me.

"You know, at least in our previous time one of us was always in our comfort zone to support the other but now we're both out of our time I feel completely lost."

"I feel the same, James. This world is not ours. I cannot latch on to anything!"

I looked closely at the screen. I could see what James meant. There was a pulse. Did it mean it was alive?

"James, it is like it is breathing."

"I need a strobe."

James rummaged around in a cupboard and brought out a tube with a lens. He connected it to a box then on pressing a button the tube emitted a flashing light. He shone the light on the diary and began to increase the rate at which the light tube flashed until it became to my eye a single beam of light.

"I'm adjusting the frequency of this strobe to see if I can match it to the pulsing of the screen."

The flickering on the screen seemed to slow down then stop for a moment before resuming at a faster speed. Then of a sudden the screen went dark. This caused a strange sensation. The room for a moment seemed different and I felt a little giddy as though my balance was upset. I reached out to James for support. He turned off the strobe and the screen lit up again and whatever I had sensed vanished.

"Did you feel or see that, Elizabeth?"

I wasn't quite sure what James meant but something had changed.

"I felt a little out of focus but I thought it was your light reflecting off the walls."

"Yeah, must have been. Wait! I think I've found the frequency of its operation. But I don't understand. Oh, of course! It's time dilation! It's not a pulsing light. Look the whole diary is oscillating in out of focus. It must be moving backwards and forwards in time!"

The screen seemed to be slowly vibrating.

"But what does that mean?" I said.

"I think it means it's not really here. It's as though it's trying to keep up with our time. Look how it shifts. It must be trying to lock onto us or something."

He turned to me.

"Elizabeth, what brought us together?"

"If you mean when we first met - why, it was our meeting at Hamgreen. Something happened which brought you back to my time."

"Or something happened which brought you and Hamgreen temporarily back to my time."

Then he turned and looked into my eyes and said something for which at this time I was not prepared.

"Elizabeth, you said you had a past. I don't know whether it's relevant to this problem but if you can bear to tell it ...."

But as I gathered my thoughts Jill appeared at the door with perfect timing.

---∼---

J.

"What the hell is going on, Jim? I could hear you from the kitchen then it all went quiet for about twenty minutes. Hello, Elizabeth. Welcome to Jim's special language laboratory."

I looked at my watch. The minute hand had moved forward about twenty minutes. Did the machine do that? Did we move forward in time? I decided to keep this to myself.

"Sorry, Jill. Just giving this box a verbal kicking."

"It didn't sound like it was your foot you were threatening it with. Anyway, so how come you both still think you're in the wrong time line? You're here at home and with your Elizabeth. Marco's stuck in the future and ComsMesh and Adcom are finished."

"Because we don't remember any of this world, do we, Elizabeth?

"I don't know, James. I was not brought up in your world so I don't know whether it's real or not."

There's nothing like support when you need it.

"God I'm beginning to doubt my sanity. Look, before Wells gave us this infernal machine there were no Air Police and no Aliens. I would've remembered, wouldn't I?"

"Well", said Jill, "this is the real world to me, Jim. If there is another Jill then knowing you she's probably fried in a nuclear war."

A thought came into my brain and came out before I could stop it

"Or you had triplets."

"I had triplets?" Said Jill and gave me a look that told me I was entering a domain where man and his humour should never tread. "Are you telling me when you persuaded me to go into that time machine I could have come out with a slack belly and a house full of kids?"

Elizabeth looked at me, then Jill and back to me. I looked

for the opening in the door.

"OK, OK, that was stupid. Sorry. Look I don't know what's real and what isn't."

Elizabeth tried to defuse the situation but unfortunately or perhaps fortunately misjudged what the fuse was attached to.

"James, you asked about my past. Why don't we look up my past to see if it matches what I remember?"

I quickly took up the diversion and looked up Elizabeth and Flory Bicester.

"It seems, Elizabeth, that you were living with a solicitor in Chi and Flory married your cousin Henry. Oh, well, there is nothing like keeping it in the family, is there?"

Elizabeth did not seem to find that funny. In fact there was cold shock on her face. I shouldn't have cracked that old joke.

I had now wound up two women. Death would be painful and slow. Then just as I braced myself for an attack on two fronts, a woman's insatiable thirst for gossip and scandal came to my rescue.

'Never mind kissing cousins", said Jill, "Elizabeth! Who is this solicitor?'

Ah, saved or so I thought.

---～---

E.

I was discovered. But how? In my world it was a secret. There had been no scandal or publicity. But here I was infamous!

They were both looking at me for an explanation although I felt that their anticipation of a reply was not completely based on judgement of my character. Nevertheless to be seen to have 'run off' with two gentlemen in my young life put me in a very delicate position. I was at a loss. I hoped James had not put me on too high a pedestal. The fall could be fatal.

Then James tried to come to my rescue.

"Jill. Don't. We've all made fools of ourselves in our lives."

"Speak for yourself, Jim."

"Yeah? What about that Tarquin in Emsworth with the yacht or the rubber dinghy, as it turned out?

"Don't you dare mention that, Jim!"

"Or that one with the villa in France or static caravan as we call it in this country. Didn't he..... ?"

"OK, OK! Alright, we are all idiots in love. I'm sorry Elizabeth I didn't mean to pry."

"It is alright Jill. But you see I am now undone."

To my surprise my words provoked a wave of sympathy in Jill who put her arm around me.

"Oh, I'm so sorry, Elizabeth, that was unforgivable of me."

"No, it has to come out, Jill. I will tell all and you can judge me."

I now stood on a road to which there was no turning back. I composed myself and began.

"I was only nineteen years of age when I met and became besotted with a gentleman of culture and wit. We would meet in Chichester and he would entertain me with marvellous stories of India and the Orient. He told me his wife had died in Jaipur which had affected him greatly and had promised himself to live a celibate life. This, as you know, Jill, becomes immediately a challenge to any woman."

"See, Jim", said Jill with that mischievous look she used with James, "all you had to do was become a monk or priest and you would have had them queuing up."

"Shall we let Elizabeth continue?"

It was a command to which she quickly acquiesced and apologised to me.

"Please do not apologise, Jill, your humour is helping. So, to continue. After our second meeting he confessed that he loved me and told me I was the sweetest thing he had ever met and I kindled such a flame in him that he wanted to live with me forever."

"Wow, Elizabeth why haven't I met a man like that? Don't answer that Jim."

"You do not want to meet a man like that, Jill, but maybe you were less naive than me at that age."

James looked perplexed. Jill said nothing save to momentarily look down at her toes. I continued.

"He tried to convince me that we should live together in a bohemian style. I was not up to do this. But I compromised. I...,"

I looked at James. I thought I saw encouragement in his eyes.

"I did spend, how can I say, some time with him in close company."

For some reason they then seemed to relax and I am sure there was almost inexplicably a look of disappointment or disinterest as though what I had done was the commonest thing in the world! I continued.

"But then I discovered he had another mistress."

Their reactions immediately changed.

"What! The bastard!" said Jill. "Did you take his eyes out?"

James concurred though suggested as men are prone to do, a more prolonged bout of violence.

I was quite taken aback by their exclamations. They do seem to use rather an extraordinary amount of vulgar language in their conversation but I could see it did have its uses in releasing suppressed emotion. I was also gratified to see that they did have some important moral boundaries.

"Yes, thank you, Jill, for expressing quite succinctly what I thought but was unable to say and although I did not take his eyes out, my hat pin did find its mark."

"Ouch!" Said James who involuntarily covered his lower half with his hands for some reason.

"Good for you Elizabeth. God, stringing along two mistresses!"

"Jill!" Said James with a look of shock on his face.

"Oops, sorry, I didn't mean to call you that."

"Yes, James, she is right. I was a mistress as well. No different from her. Except, she was a married woman! When I found out I was heartbroken. I immediately stopped seeing him. I was such a fool!"

"And did anyone find out?" Said Jill.

"No, only Flory who gave me great sympathy and support and kept it a secret. So you see my manners and position which I have shown you are a sham. But now I find I am a mistress again and my former secret is in the papers!"

Jill could see I was almost in tears and hugged me closer. She turned to James.

"Say something, Jim!"

I looked at James. I awaited his judgement.

---~---

J.

I could see what this confession had cost her and also that she regarded herself as my mistress which compromised her honour and increased her vulnerability. I realised the time had come to do what I had promised to do.

I got down on one knee and held her hand. It was a moment I would remember as I had managed to place my knee rather excruciatingly on a drawing pin which I must have swept off the desk during one of my discussions with the diary. I desperately hoped the pain on my face and the tightness of my hand on hers would be interpreted as my affection for her.

"Elizabeth, will you marry me?"

"Blooming hell!" said Jill. "Where's my camera? This is going straight in the family album. Keep still, Jim, and keep that expression. Elizabeth, move round a bit so I can get your profile. Perfect."

"Jill!"

"Yes, Jim? Changed your mind?"

"Will you please shut up and let Elizabeth speak? I've got a drawing pin stuck in my knee and I can't keep this position much longer. Aagh!"

And what did they do? They both fell about laughing. Jeez, only 20 minutes ago I was happily alone working on that confounded diary and now I found myself proposing marriage with a spike in my knee with two witless females bent on ..!

Then Elizabeth took pity on me, well, eventually, helped me up and pulled out the pin from my knee.

"Of course I will marry you, James," she kissed me quickly and said, "And I will keep this as a remembrance of this moment and the sacrifice you made for me." A bit more sincerity would have been welcome.

God! You try to be romantic with a girl and look what happens. I made a mental note to burn every Bronte and Austen book in the house. Then Jill said: "Here Elizabeth let me take a pic of your memento. Oh my God, Jim, look you're bleeding!" But instead of attending to the injury, "nurse" Jill took a picture of my bloody trousers and turning said, "Well, Elizabeth, there can't be many men who would shed blood to get a girl's hand in marriage"

Then they were off on their merriment train again.

"This bleeding proposal will be off if you two don't stop laughing."

Of course they didn't and I didn't withdraw my offer.

---〜---

E.

We were married the following week. James had done his best to recreate my world. He had dug out a series of pre-Raphaelite prints in the hope that they would be to my liking from which I chose for my wedding dress that of Ophelia painted by Waterhouse. I do not know how much it cost. James chose a complete highland outfit in the tartan of the hunting Urquhart. He looked very fetching.

He found for our ceremony an enchanted dell of yew near my home at Hamgreen and festooned it with flowers and garlands. I had wanted to be married in a church but when he showed me what he had prepared for me I felt that if God was to agree to a marriage between James and a fallen woman he would approve of this place for our binding. For as James said, although he was not a religious man he thought if God exists then surely to be married in a place of his creation was preferable to one of man's. When I saw the bower I could not disagree.

---~---

Out of Time

Chapter Thirteen

J.

Happiest man in the world and all that; best day of my life, etc. Marrying Elizabeth was the best thing I have ever done, and so on.

---~---

J.

A day or so later, I was back in the attic with the diary trying to understand time dilation. What was causing it? Perhaps it was really out of time. For some reason I tried weighing it. Yes it had weight. Then I realised that was a pointless exercise as I didn't know what it was supposed to weigh. I wished I could talk to Wells. I was in his time line but which one? Perhaps the clue was in one of his books. Or perhaps the diary was just the manifestation of something bigger in our time or possibly some other time. There must be a key. A key? Perhaps it would respond to a musical note or scale?

I picked up my guitar and played C Major Scale. Then I tried the minor. The E$\flat$ caused a slight change in colour. I tried the chromatic scale across three octaves. B$\flat$, A$\flat$ changed the colour.

I picked up the strobe light again and tuned the flash frequency to B$\flat$ and shone it at the screen. The screen turned black. Then for some reason, possibly because I had been watching the strobe too closely, I had the distinct impression that the room blurred again! I switched it off immediately and the room bounced or wobbled back into shape. I needed a rest. My eyes were aching. But I felt I was close to something. I called Elizabeth.

"Elizabeth! Come quick I think I've cracked it."

She came up the ladder and I explained what I had done.

"Are you sure your language has not just shamed it into giving up its secrets?"

"Watch." I said, ignoring her jibe, and turned on the strobe. The screen went black. The room began to mist over again. Then I swear strange shapes or shadows began to appear out of the walls.

"Stop it, James! Please!"

I turned it off.

The shadows disappeared.

"You saw something too?"

"The room seemed to flicker, James, and it made me feel unsteady."

"I think this diary is just the front end of something else. Are you prepared to explore?"

"Explore what, James? Do you not think we have explored enough in our short time together? You have not been reading by chance the Strange Adventures of Captain Dangerous and let his exploits put foolish ideas in your head?"

"Captain Dangerous?" This chap seemed to be one up on my self-appointment as Captain Intrepid.

"You have not heard of GAS, James? You know Augustus Sala. I thought he was all the rage amongst young men who preferred their adventures from the comfort of an armchair."

"Ah, these days we get our kicks from a comfy seat at the cinema. Besides, you may have noticed I don't look for adventure. Adventure seems to find me! And as soon as I can finish this damn adventure and get back to my cottage and armchair the better."

She held my hand. "OK, James, I see you are in earnest but please do not let go of me!"

I turned on the strobe. The screen went dark and the room

shimmered. I felt her hand tighten around mine. I turned to her. The hairs on the back of my neck tingled. Ripples of light were passing through her body. She was growing faint, no, she was becoming transparent. What was happening? Then my desk began to dissolve before my eyes. I tried to grab my chair but felt nothing. I could still feel Elizabeth's hand but when I looked down our hands and more importantly the strobe had vanished!

What I thought were flickering shadows began to form shapes. The walls expanded at an incredible speed dragging the shapes and shadows with them until suddenly there was a shift in my vision and I found myself floating in what seemed to be the ruins of a great gothic cathedral. It was bathed in a green glow. Vines grew and clung to the walls, and above, white ancient towers broken by time reached for the sky. With some trepidation I slowly looked downwards. Fear washed over me. My body had disappeared! I turned to Elizabeth. She was gone! Yet I could feel her hand in mine. I had a sensation of floating or drifting invisibly. I looked down further and to my horror I realised there was a graveyard below me which covered the floor of the nave. What looked like broken crosses, stooping angels and mausoleums lay in rows, covered with blue-grey, iridescent, mildew. Hooded creatures like bats drifted over the stones. I was immersed in a gothic horror.

"Elizabeth!" I shouted. I did not hear my voice but I heard it in my head. Then dozens of girlish faint voices percolated into my mind like sprites.

"Oh where am I? Where is James? I am lost. No! My God, I know this place! Hold me, James!"

I shouted in my head. "I'm here, Elizabeth." Wherever here was.

Then the intimate warmth of Elizabeth suddenly enveloped my senses. Oh, what bliss.

"Oh, James. I can feel you but I can't see you". Then a sharp sound. "Oh, you can't think about sex now, surely?" Before I could reply her voice changed. "Oh, James." She came closer. I could smell her scent and sweet breath. Her voice whispered, "Oh, that is so nice." She was melting into me.

I had to get out of this. We were drowning in pleasure. I tried to will myself into other thoughts. I felt a jolt.

"James, why are you thinking about your mother!!" Her warmth withdrew immediately. "Oh, I see. I will also try to keep similar thoughts in my head."

I could not see what distracted her but some semblance of normality returned though her confused thoughts kept on entering my head. Some not as complimentary as I would have liked. She sensed it. A flood of disjointed telepathic words entered my mind.

"Oh, why did I agree....Oh, I'm sorry, James, we are feeling all our thoughts. We must get out before we find out everything about each other. Yes, I know you don't know how.... Who is Captain Intrepid? Oh I see... You are not a failure... Yes, that is how I see you....oh, is that how you see me? Oh, that is so nice....I'm falling into you again...must think of something else quick."

---∼---

E.

For a brief moment it was like a dream of a familiar place to which I could not remember. The great nave rose up above me and opened to the sky. It was beautiful. I was floating free in the air without my body but I was inside my mind and then the enormity of what had happened struck me. Where was James? I reached out for him. My thoughts like sprites flew from my mind, searching.

Then his thoughts washed across me like waves. Some just ripples and others, though thankfully few, like storm waves crashing against a cliff. I tried to cushion myself from them but to no avail. I had not realised what passion a man had for a woman's body, nor how it could provoke such an equally passionate response! How manners and conventions suppressed our evolutionary urges to procreate and survive. Though I imagine without them we would still be living in caves. I could see why some species were seasonal in their amorous relationships.

I had to think and help James.

"James, James! Can you feel the strobe?"

The word "feel" made him press against me then he withdrew.

"I'm trying."

"Try imagining it your hand, oh, and try to imagine <u>that</u> is not in your hand. Really, James!"

"Sorry. Yes, I can feel it. I'm going to press it."

The cathedral vanished. We were in James' attic again.

"My God, Elizabeth. I apologise for every thought I had about you."

Actually, I was very flattered. Imagine if he had been false in his love for me. But I must not let him ascend too far above me.

"Well, James, at least I have a better understanding of men when they offer me their affections."

He looked mortified. How vulnerable men are constantly needing compliments on their devotions. Then he caught me.

"And how many "understandings" have you had Elizabeth?"

Had he seen inside my mind? Did he know my whole life? What had the diary done? What had he seen? I involuntarily put up my wall and prepared my arrows. He saw it.

Out of Time

--- 〜 ---

J.

Why did I say that? I can sit down and use orthogonal Eigen vectors, almost imagine 4D space and solve the equations to get a space ship to Pluto. Yet a simple inquiry into a girl's past life... Oh dear.

"Am I dead now, Elizabeth?"

"No, James, but I have sharpened my arrows."

I winced.

" Feel free to keep that arrow and if you think I'm going to say something like that again please prod me sharply with it."

"Oh, James, you do test me at times but we have just experienced more intimacy than possibly any other couple have had and survived. You could have submerged me in your mind and done with me what you will. To resist that is love indeed."

If only she knew how close I had been to not resisting. I tried to move on.

"So what happened?" That was supposed to be rhetorical.

"We have been back and forth in time, James. We have jumped to a new time and now we have gone out of time."

We had jumped out of time. I thought about this. But it had not been our corporeal selves. Where we had been had been without mass and without mass we had been able to leave time! We had entered the realms of light!

Just then Jill came up the ladder.

"Oh, that's where you are. Where have you been for the last two days? You could have told me you were going away. I could have arranged a nice private party with Sean."

I looked at her then Elizabeth.

"We've been here all the time Jill. In fact we were only talking to you about an hour ago."

Out of Time

"What - you've found another time machine?"

"No we've found a non-time machine. A machine where time stands still."

$$---\sim---$$

Out of Time

Chapter Fourteen

J,

The next day I was back in the attic with Elizabeth. We had been writing notes of our experience for over an hour trying to make sense of it but to avail.

"Are you prepared to go back, Elizabeth? We'll have to concentrate very hard but I've got the strobe to get us back out."

"I don't know, James. We are too close. Suppose we cannot resist each other? We would fall into an infinite abyss of passion."

I could think of worse ways of dying and I wondered how long I could last.

But before I could reply she picked up the strobe and placed it my hand. Then she took my thumb and putting hers over mine pressed the button. We and the room began to fade again. Her aroma grew stronger and we were in the cathedral again. Now what? We needed to get closer. I willed myself to move and to my surprise the nave drifted towards us. I looked down at the graveyard. There were the creatures again. As I tried to discern what they were, to my horror we found ourselves descending towards them! I was moving by thought.

Suddenly I saw a movement in the graveyard. Something larger than the creatures slowly rose like a ghost towards us. A blue glow surrounded it which added to the ghoulish atmosphere. As it came closer I could see it was dressed in some sort of Victorian garb with winged collar and a cravat or bow. Its hair or as I now realised, his hair, for I could see it was in the shape of a man, was mysteriously blowing in a non-existent wind. I kept my thumb poised over what I hoped was the strobe button. Elizabeth in her fear had melted into me. We were both one. I did not know whether she was me or I was her.

Then a wave of Elizabeth's raw emotions of fear, a child's fear, like a hot breath washed over me. Her thoughts shouted at me and echoed in my mind. I felt her thumb press on mine but I resisted.

"Press the button, James, PLEASE! I cannot cope. It is a thing of the Night Mare!"

But I was riveted to the spot. He rose higher. All my childhood fears of the night flooded back. The creak of the stairs. A dark figure by the door. A memory of floating down a staircase. A long staircase vanishing into the darkness except now there was this phantom rising up towards me. As he got closer I noticed he seemed to be trying to walk or swim through an invisible treacle. His eyes moved left and right as though trying to grasp its surrounds. Then I felt him sense me. Sweat was running down my face. Elizabeth was sobbing. I felt her breath on my neck. His eyes, then his face, turned towards me. There was something familiar about it.

Suddenly Elizabeth's voice stung my mind "It's Wells, James!"

Before I could reply his voice came. I recognised the clipped accent.

"Ah! I found you. Are you Elizabeth Bicester and James Urquhart? Ah, yes, you are. Please! Concentrate! I can't stay long. I am drifting out of your space-time... Yes of course you have the conduit, yes, that electric diary.... Please calm down. Your thoughts are drowning me."

Elizabeth and I were now just one confused mind of jumbled thoughts. We were going out of control again but this time we were falling into an abyss of fear.

His voice came again. "It is no good. You are not strong enough. This will not do. I will scribe in the diary then you must let go... Yes it is done... Go, go quickly! You cannot stay here!"

I didn't need further encouragement. I pressed the strobe button, he and the cathedral vanished and we were in the attic. I was drenched in sweat. Elizabeth was, erm, glowing is the correct term, I think.

"James, the dogs of hell could not drag me back to that ghoulish place. I feel, oh dear, I am quite weak, I thought I had entered Hell before my time!"

I took hold of her. I could feel the moisture through her clothes. God knows what she thought I felt like.

"Christ, Elizabeth, I am drained. When you don't believe in ghosts and then you think you've met one. God, I thought my heart was going to explode with fright."

"Oh, James, we have gone beyond the realms of our imagination. And whoever said two minds are better than one has obviously not tried it! We are too alike. Oh, I must rest before I faint!"

I held her closely. Her breast pulsated against mine. We needed to get out of the attic. "Let's go and have a cup of tea."

We went downstairs. I was still shaking. Jill was in the kitchen.

"God, you gave me a fright. You'll have to stop this, you two. That's four days this time. It wouldn't be so bad if I knew when you were coming back." Then she noticed our state.

"Gosh, what have you being doing? You both look like you've been at it like rabbits again." She saw my look.

"O, so what happened this time?"

---~---

E.

The reference to James, I and rabbits, was a little uncalled for and the word 'again' also caused me some consternation but after my recent confessions I felt it best not to protest. Nevertheless, it served to take the edge off our adventure and return some normality, if there was any normality to be found in this world.

"We have been closer than you might think, Jill, and if you had seen what we have just experienced…..." I stopped. I could see by her mischievous expression that she was purposely misinterpreting me. "Jill!" I said. "We have been through hell!" Then I felt faint again. Jill came to my assistance

"You poor girl, sit down. Would you like a cup of tea? Jim, what have you done to her?"

We sat down and after two large cups of tea served without saucers we related our experience and our brief meeting with Mr Wells.

"My God, what's it like being in each other's minds? That must have been a test, Elizabeth, what's it like being in Jim's head? Is it really just empty save for a small box of sexual innuendos?"

"Dear Jill, the intense emotional effect was so strong that I fear that even the rabbits to which you referred would have found it hard to keep up."

This provoked a sudden burst of laughter from both of them which I had not expected and left me momentarily nonplussed until looking at Jill's expression of mock surprise I realised I had inadvertently contributed another innuendo. These free conversations on sex I do find a little trying to participate and Jill does so catch me off guard.

And James didn't help by suggesting "You could run a comedy show, Elizabeth. With your diction and straight face you would have them in stitches! Your Sister Flory said it was as easy as game pie to make you fall into a trap".

"Flory! I will have words with her if I see her again. It is a bit much to find one cannot take refuge in one's own family; James, you are taking too much advantage of me! It is not sport to take advantage of a lady with a reputation to uphold."

At that point I raised a white flag as both their expressions seem to have a questioning attitude towards what reputation I was trying to uphold and so I joined in the humour; for I could see that they meant well and it was I admit a welcome relief from our recent experiences.

Luckily James diverted the conversation, "It was pure emotion, Jill. Almost more than we could handle but the real question is what was Wells doing there?"

"I do not know what he was doing there but I do know where that ruin is." I said.

"What!" They said in unison.

"It is the Abbey of the White Monks at Rievaulx in North Yorkshire. I am almost sure. For I have vague memories as a child visiting a great house near Helmsley and visiting the Castle and the Abbey"

And then I remembered what Wells had said.

"James! Wells said he had scribed something in the diary."

---~---

J.

I retrieved the diary from the attic. The screen was blank. I pressed it and the following words appeared.

'Two ways. Your dimensions or the diary. There are four. Rievaulx, Fountains, Jervaulx and Bylands."

I looked up. "Aren't these all abbeys, Elizabeth? Any idea what's special about them?"

"I do not know, James, but I believe they are all in the North

Riding and built by the Cistercians."

"Mmh! as you thought you recognised Rievaulx we'll go there first in the hope we'll make sense of what we saw."

I was exhausted and protested.

"Please, James, I need to rest and if I am not being too indelicate, my clothes after that experience would not be fit for a Poor House laundry."

"Don't worry we'll wait 'till tomorrow."

And Jill said. "As for your clothes you still have all those bought in Chi at Jim's expense."

I quickly displayed my empty wallet. No sympathy. Then a thought struck me.

"On the question of clothes I think we must pack for the 19th century."

"Why, James?"

"Well, from whatever was going on in that cathedral it was in that century and I'm going to make sure I've got the right money and clothes with me this time just in case we end up there."

Elizabeth came close to me. There was fear in her face.

"Please, James, tell me we are not going back via that diary."
"Quite right, Elizabeth. We'll take a plane."

---~---

E.

I stood in a bright white hall, the size of a cathedral. Hundreds of people milled around me. It reminded me of St Pancras on the weekend of the newly introduced Bank Holiday or St. Lubock's Day as it was popularly referred to by the working classes.

James was rather taken aback by the size of my luggage and blamed Jill quite unfairly in advising what I should take. He was good enough to carry most of it though not without comment.

"Are you sure you have bought enough there, Elizabeth?" Said James lifting my five bags into a cart. I played him.

"No, James, I have left three hat boxes behind as Jill said that you had your limits in this area."

Poor man did look suitably shocked.

"Actually I was more worried how Easyjet was going to fit it all in the hold and how many passengers would have to be left behind."

"A lady requires a lot of effort to be acceptable in polite company."

"But with your natural looks, Elizabeth, I didn't know effort was required." Before I bit he gave a smile that indicated he appreciated how much effort I had put in and proceeded to push my luggage along the hall. In this world compliments to a lady are so different but so much more rewarding.

We passed on our luggage to the female porter at the baggage reception who on regarding my items gave a surprised look similar to James and I'm sure almost took pity on him before she caught my eye. Then we went to the main hall for embarkation. It was almost the size of one of the new London train termini. On one side great windows almost thirty feet square, perfectly transparent and without blemish, allowed a view of the white and coloured sleek birds I had often seen flying high up in the evening sky. I cannot describe their size with their enormous wings swept back waiting in rows but I think the great transatlantic steamers I had seen on occasion at Southampton would compare. Then one began to move. It trundled across the field like a great beast and came to a halt. Then as though briefly surveying its surrounds it unleashed an immense hidden power which caused it to accelerate. I had expected steam or a rocket trail but saw nothing. Faster and faster it went until I became convinced that this great bird would never leave the ground. But just as I had almost given up hope and that it would end in a terrible accident, to my relief its nose lifted towards the sky and it rose from the ground so slowly that I thought it must still crash but up and up it went, until sharply turning, disappeared into the clouds.

I was much concerned that I might not survive travelling at such a speed for I had learnt that planes travel ten times faster than James' carriage! Would the air keep up? Would we be able to speak or would our voices be left behind? And they fly so high that apparently if one went outside one would either freeze to death or die of asphyxiation for lack of air! I was not reassured by James telling me not to worry as passengers were prohibited from leaving the plane whilst flying. Soon it was our turn. James took me down a tunnel with dozens of other people. Some were with children who I could see were very excited at the prospect of flying and seemed to view being catapulted into the sky as fun as visiting a Steam Fair. I resolved to be brave as them. But then children always think they are immortal. At the end of the tunnel was a door which I quickly realised was the entrance to our plane. The noise from what I took to be the engines was almost deafening. A uniformed usherette wearing more paint on her face than she probably needed showed us in. The inside of the plane was like a cylindrical tube with dozens of seats with a small passageway between them. Some were already occupied. I held James hand tightly for I was feeling a little claustrophobic.

We found two narrow chairs amongst a group who judging by their accents, manners and beachwear had come from one of the northern industrial towns and had overindulged on a trip to the seaside. Their familiarity was quite trying but thankfully humorous though their compliments towards me were rather direct. When they saw me blush after one rather crude innuendo, one suggested that James should take me for a 'good night' in Hartlepool which would ensure that I never blushed again. I looked at James for support who at first reassured me by saying that he had no intention of ever going to Hartlepool with me but then joined in the 'banter' by saying he was going to take me for a 'good night' in Helmsley instead!

I would seriously advise any other ladies from my time who find themselves stranded in this world to abandon all hope of finding a chivalrous gentleman who would defend her honour.

I asked James if he could afford to move to a first-class compartment to which one of the party who overheard replied in their peculiar vernacular.

"You're already in it, pet."

At this point I had to laugh for I could now see there was no class at all.

James had sat me next to a porthole through which I could see the outside world. I could feel the noise of the engines and strange mechanical movements below me though I noticed no one was worried. Just as I had almost convinced myself that I would be safe, to my horror one of the uniformed usherettes decided to explain to us what do if we fell out of the sky! Why she wanted to remind us of what I feared the most I do not know. I listened intently but to my surprise she did not dwell on how to arrest a fall but on what to do in the unlikely event that one landed and survived such a disaster. She then pointed to two small doors through which we could escape if such an event occurred. The operation of opening the doors suggested it required a man of herculean strength which looked beyond the powers of the frail gentleman sitting next to them. Then when she produced a small yellow bag and told us it was an aid to buoyancy if we fell in the sea I began to suspect that this was some macabre amusement to test our mettle. This was reinforced by the complete absence of any fear or even, incredibly, any interest in this performance amongst the passengers and led me to the conclusion that either everyone had volunteered for the Suicide Express or such disasters were a rarity.

I looked out of the porthole for distraction and had a weird sensation that the buildings outside were beginning to move! I grabbed James' hand before I realised rather foolishly that it was us. Lights flashed, bells rang and a sign appeared telling us not to smoke. Why anyone would think of smoking a cigar at this moment and in such a confined space I have no idea. Then James told me to sit back in my seat and 'relax' for we were about to 'take off'. His checking of the strap across my waist did not aid my relaxation. I was conscious that I was squeezing his hand very tight. Suddenly the noise of the engines started to grow louder and louder. I closed my eyes tight. The engines sounded like they would explode. What power is needed to lift into the sky such a gigantic bird? Then we started to move faster and faster. I could not believe the speed. The plane started to shake. I opened my eyes momentarily and saw buildings and planes rushing past. Then the wings changed shape! But before I could say anything an invisible hand pushed me back into the chair. My head pressed against the cushion. I could not move! What incredible force held me? Buildings flashed by. I was almost convinced that we would not lift off the ground and end in a mangled death but then we began to rise leaving the ground. My stomach churned. If someone had told me I was on a charabanc that had shot in the air and detached itself from its moorings I would believe it.

Then, Oh my god! I was leaving the earth! I forced myself to look out the window. The land, the houses, dropped away becoming smaller and smaller. What speed were we going? I looked up and could see clouds then wisps of mist fly past us which grew thicker until we were in a complete fog. How could the driver see for I could see nothing? Suddenly the plane almost turned on its side. There were mechanical noises and the sound of groaning metal. My stomach churned again. Just as I thought we were really going to meet our maker a little earlier than expected, I was floating above the clouds and the invisible force pressing me into my chair abated. I ventured to look out. There was nothing below me save white fleeced clouds scurrying across tiny fields and hedgerows and up above a blue, sunlit sky. I was flying like a bird! Oh, who would imagine such a thing could really happen? I was a wondrous child. What power had been harnessed?

We were floating far above a sea of clouds. An immense calm came over me. I felt we were on a sailing ship or a balloon. Only the occasional tiny silver bird darting across the sky reminded me what speed we were travelling.

The landing of the plane, however, I prefer not to describe for we descended for what seemed an eternity through a thick fog and the only indication that we had returned safely to Mother Earth was an almighty jolt followed by much pitching about which gave me the distinct impression we were all riding a gigantic Wiz Bang set off by a malevolent, demonic child. If this was not enough to make me think about my Maker we suddenly all lurched forward to a stop as though we had hit the buffers at the end of a train station! This was met by spontaneous cheering from the passengers which suggested that falling out of the sky was not as rare as James had implied.

We were the last to leave the plane. The fog enveloped us affording no view through the port hole.

Apparently we had arrived or should I say dropped out of the sky at a place called Durham-Tees Valley. James said its only claim to fame was that it wasn't in Durham or in a valley

The usherette waved goodbye and hoped we would come again. I thanked her for her offer though with not much conviction. We walked down a steep portable stair case on to a wide concrete surface. The other passengers must have gone ahead for we found ourselves on our own. Our luggage was waiting for us at the bottom of the steps.

I commented that I was surprised there were no porters to help us,

"That's weird," said James, "There's usual a truck to carry the bags to the terminal. Perhaps there wasn't room for all yours."

"Perhaps that's the price one must pay for not travelling first class."

Before James could reply I said, "However as no porters are to be found we must carry them ourselves."

James did his best to carry what I thought was his fair share.

The fog was thick upon the ground. I could not see the other passengers but I could just see a building ahead of us. It looked remarkably like a provincial train station.

.

As we approached the building I was sure I could smell something familiar to me. I asked James.

"I think it's the local farmers muck spreading."

"No, James, something else." Then I remembered - it was steam, the smell of a steam engine.

We were back in the nineteenth century but in the wrong clothes!

---~---

Out of Time

Chapter Fifteen

E.

I never thought when I first met James on that cricket field at Hamgreen that it would result in finding myself in a coal yard at the back of a train station in a state of considerable undress with him in a similar state trying to change our clothes. I can only tell you that the thought of being caught by the local constabulary wearing a modern skirt which reached only to my knees spurred me on. Thank God for the fog!

This time travel might sound like a wondrous adventure but one needs to be prepared to abandon all modesty when the need arises.

---∼---

J.

I was quite surprised how quickly Elizabeth was prepared to remove her clothes when the need arose, though I kept that thought to myself.

---∼---

E.

We dressed as well we could given the limited facilities available in a coal yard. I had not been able to arrange my bustle properly which gave me more of the look of a country girl and I had also forgone a corset. However I was reassured by James who had found a scrap of newspaper which suggested we were in 1895 and was able to point out that bustles were not as popular in society at this time. I would have been surprised at his knowledge of such things if Jill had not told me recently at one of our afternoon teas while James was working in his attic or his 'shed upstairs' as she called it, that he had taken quite an 'interest' in understanding the 'workings' of Victorian ladies' clothing during the early days of our courting.

Too late I realised I had forgotten a mirror.

"James, is my face clean of soot? I would not want to be regarded as a blackamoor."

"No, your face is clean. However, when we get back to my time we may have to have a discussion on how things have changed with regard to our attitudes to the people of your Empire."

"Ah, yes. I understand. I'm sorry. Old habits are difficult to change. However, I do feel I need to powder my face."

"I could do it for you."

"Thank you, James. I don't want to question your skills in this area but I do not want to be regarded as a mad clown who has escaped from the local circus."

"Then how about we pass ourselves off as missionaries? I believe the wives are usually quite sparing with the makeup."

This seemed a passable idea until I remembered and pointed out that there were not many openings for missionaries in my age for those who had not read the bible, could not speak a word of Latin and had a questioning attitude towards God's existence.

Thankfully James persisted.

"How about we said we had an accident and were late for the train?"

Looking at the amount of coal dust I had attracted this seemed better.

"Yes. We will fabricate a story that the wheel fell off the cart and we had to run for the train."

The list of virtues I had abandoned was getting longer.

---∼---

J.

I managed to get two tickets for Thirsk, first class with a change at Northallerton. I was really looking forward to this.

It was like getting on the Pickering steam railway. I could even hear that long forgotten rhythmic clickity click, clickity click of the rails. The carriage had upholstered seats and unlike the second-class carriages it had glazed windows which you could open and hang your head out of. Elizabeth advised against this as it usually resulted in a covering of soot. This was not going to stop me fulfilling a childhood dream. However, the blast of steam and soot was quite surprising. On withdrawing my head, Elizabeth felt she had to comment.

'Why, James, you seem to have received an extraordinary amount of soot, which I presume by its mixture with the hot vapour emanating from the chimney has caused it to adhere to your visage and clothes quite wondrously."

'Yes, Elizabeth," looking at myself, "and if I may attempt your vernacular: one notices one is alone in a carriage, which is not expected to halt for another half an hour, with a lady who in one's humble opinion needs 'a good seeing to'."

"Oh, Sir. How could a lady resist a man who demonstrates his intentions with such poetic language?" She demurely leant back into the upholstery and revealed a beautifully embroidered, red stockinged, calf. "But pray tell me, Sir what shall we do with the other twenty minutes?"

I began to suspect that those afternoon tea conversations with my sister were not entirely about flower arranging.

The other twenty minutes, by the way, were used in frantically removing as much soot and coal dust as possible from our clothes and carriage before we arrived at Northallerton.

---~---

E.

On the train to Thirsk we shared a compartment with a couple of a similar age. They were much concerned about our unlucky 'accident' and how James had received blotches of soot on his face and collar. James was reticent to recount how he had arrived at this condition so I helped by saying that despite my advice he had wished to get a better view of the countryside from our carriage. We ladies then exchanged some pleasantries on how men never grow up but I went no further when James, who by now had felt that I had taken too much advantage, whispered that he was quite happy to draw attention to the spots of coal dust and sooty hand marks on my jacket and blouse and how they got there.

Having heard our 'story' the lady then produced a knapsack from which she offered some game pie. I had to help James resist taking too much. We found during our conversation that they were spending a few days touring the Yorkshire Moorlands ghost hunting which I remembered had recently become very popular. James attracted much interest though not necessarily credulity by suggesting they visit Loch Ness where he assured them he had personally seen the Loch Ness Monster.

We then enquired whether they knew anything of the folklore of Rievaulx and they told us sometimes the bells were heard at midnight. But they were more interested in Helmsley Castle where a mysterious green lady had been reported and also pixies seen dancing in the grounds.

--- ~ ---

J.

These stories of ghosts were interesting. Though I hoped no one noticed Elizabeth's embroidered green skirts and jacket and made a connection.

When we got to Thirsk Elizabeth arranged what is called a Hansom Cab to take us to Helmsley though when it turned up I couldn't see anything handsome about it. It looked like it had been retrieved from a swamp and the nags look like they would welcome being shot. Even Elizabeth felt that it wasn't quite what she expected and likened it to a dog cart.

I don't know whether you have been up Sutton Bank in a dog cart but I think even dogs would refuse the journey. It was not helped by Elizabeth enjoying the view and pointing out the steep cliffs and lake below. I found myself holding her quite tight which she took to advantage and said,

"James, this is very cosy is it not and you hold me so nicely considering the distraction of the precipices and the ruts in this steep road, not to mention the age of the driver and the squeaking wheel on your side. But even with the White Horse above to aid a romantic frolic, I feel this is too a public place to encourage your amorous advances."

I love her.

---~---

E.

Poor James. He does allow me to tease him so. We took a room in the Coaching Inn at Helmsley. The landlord was just generous enough to not comment on our attire or virtue, though his wife regarded me with a look that only a woman brought up steeped in Calvinistic values and abstinence can give to another. She reminded me of the old spinsters and widows who lunch in the dining rooms of Chichester and who claim they have forsaken men but in truth it is men who have forsaken them.

But to Rievaulx which unfortunately for James required another dog cart. He did not seem too enthusiastic so I offered him a horse.

Out of Time

--- ~ ---

J.

Up to now my only experience of riding horses was pony trekking in the Brecon Beacons where the stupid nag I was on decided that it had got lost and proceeded to gallop (or canter as I later found out) across the bogs looking for its mates! The lack of synchronisation between the rising and falling of my backside and the saddle affected my gait for quite a few days afterwards and made me realise why cowboys walk the way they do.

Now I was going to get on a real horse. It was big. No, it was gigantic and by its look, hated me. The stable lad's smirk when I asked for assistance indicated he had nearly correctly guessed I was some Londoner who had come out to try the countryside to impress his new wife. Once I got the right foot in the stirrup it only took him three attempts to get me over the saddle. This was watched with some amusement, but also I was grateful to see a little sympathy, by Elizabeth who was already sitting comfortably in her saddle and whispering sweet nothings to her horse which seemed, unaccountably, to have adopted her as a lifelong friend.

If we get back I'm going to take her bungee jumping or white-water rafting... and in her Victorian underwear!

--- ~ ---

E.

I had to hold James reins to get him up the hill. I hoped we did not meet any people on the way as he had given up with the reins and had his arms wrapped tightly around the horse's neck. I must admit I had expected more courage. Though perhaps this was a price we must pay for increased equality between the sexes. I mentioned this to James and qualified it by saying from my limited experience it was a price worth paying. This mollified him somewhat though he could not be persuaded to adopt a position more fitting to a gentleman escorting his wife for a pleasant ride in the countryside.

---~---

J.

We arrived at the Cistercian ruins about lunch time and had more delicious game pie at a cottage nearby. Elizabeth had tethered the horses for us and obtained fodder for them for a few pence. I hadn't even thought about feeding them and her action had reminded me how far my world had left the natural world.

The Abbey hadn't changed at all. It stood in a secluded wood, quietly away from the world. I was still walking like I had been doing the splits and was wondering whether my thighs would ever meet again.

"Are you OK, James?"

"Yes, but if you're thinking about starting a family, could you hold off for a couple of days?"

"I'm surprised, James. In my day the heroine of popular books was always ravished after the hero returned from a good ride."

My look stopped her.

"I've managed to do it again haven't I, James?"

"Yes, I love it. However, I'm thinking that we would both welcome a returning home that avoided horses and planes. Anyway, let's have a look at this Abbey."

---~---

E.

There was definitely a similarity between this abbey and the one we found with the diary except there were no gravestones.

James said. "Let's have a look at the diary. Perhaps it will respond here."

There was nothing unusual.

"Perhaps you should have brought your flashing light."

"I have." And to my amazement he produced it from his pocket.

We stood together in the nave holding each other's hand. James played the light on the diary. The surrounds shimmered. I knew there was no going back.

--- ∼ ---

Out of Time

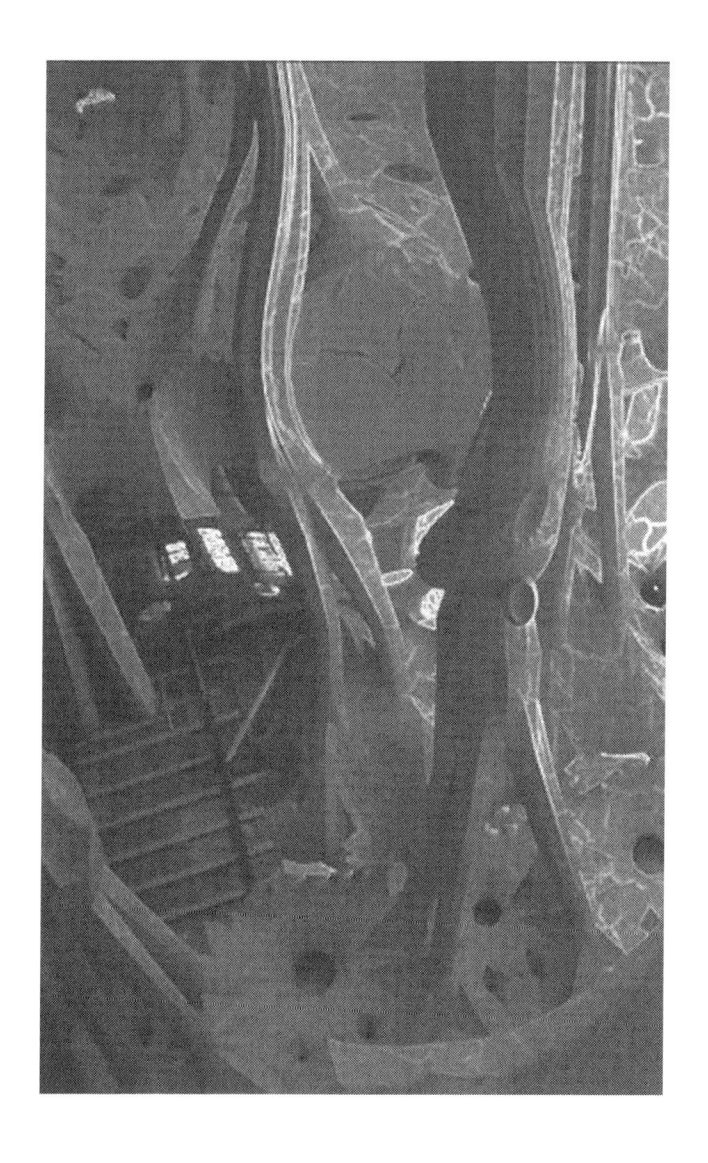

Chapter Sixteen

J.

"God! What are we doing here?"

We were in the middle of the courtyard of Helmsley Castle in the company of five sheep. The ruins of the keep towered above us. Near the entrance were a few people, some of whom looked like tourists. I pointed them out to Elizabeth.

"Do you think this is still the 1890s?"

"Their clothes do suggest we are still in the 1890s though I cannot account for the fashions in Yorkshire. Two of them do seem to be wearing the sporting clothes of Mr Burberry which were popular in Surrey in my time."

"And still are, Elizabeth. In fact, in my time when you're in the countryside that's how you can tell people are from Surrey."

As I looked around the castle wondering what I should be looking for I noticed she was looking at me rather strangely.

"James, there is something different?"

I quickly scanned around me. The sheep were still contently grazing. "What is it?"

"We are still in our bodies and standing on terra firma."

I looked down and then at her. I touched her hand. She was right. We weren't an ethereal projection. We were actually here. The diary had transported us physically to Helmsley!

"This is madness. We seem to have no control over this blooming thing what so ever."

"I know James, but as we have been brought here by this infernal machine, I suggest we take advantage of the evening light and explore."

Oh dear. Time to get Captain Intrepid out again. I hope she hadn't noticed how battered he was looking.

We went up to the keep and entered. I could tell by the absence of guard rails and ropes and the presence of abundant vegetation not to mention shrubs growing out of the moss-covered walls and floors that it hadn't had the benefit yet of an English Heritage makeover.

There was nothing unusual so we agreed during another moment of what I can only describe in hindsight as an attack of collective brain fever, to try the diary with the strobe again. I realised we really didn't know what we were doing any more. Once again we held hands, hoping against hope that we would find ourselves back in my cosy attic again.

The room shimmered and the walls and floor looked a little smoother than before but now from above a green glow could be seen. As our cerebral delirium had not subsided we found ourselves floating? up the stairs to explore its origins. I tried not to think about the absence of handrails and the rather nasty drop to the ground below if we slipped. I hid my fear by constantly asking Elizabeth if she was OK. I hoped she was embellishing the truth as much as I was. At the top we entered a large hall where there was a large bulbous vessel which judging by its size had not arrived via the door. As we stood there I thought I could hear a faint humming sound though I couldn't identify its source. A green glow similar to what we had seen through the diary at Rievaulx emanated from the machine illuminating the room. But what awoke a cold fear in me was the three articulated joints and legs supporting it.

"I know what this is, Elizabeth. What's it doing here and in this time?"

"I do not know, James. But if it is one of those hateful monstrous Martian Tripods, I think we should leave quietly."

This was just the kind of encouragement I hoped for in a girl. We went down the slippery staircase as fast and as quietly as fear of falling would allow. Captain Intrepid was firmly back in his box and the lid closed and locked.

But as we descended the stone stairs to the cellar, the humming became inexplicably louder. And it was coming from the ground. At the base the floor was now smooth, like metal; I tried it with my foot. It was solid. For some reason, which still escapes me and is still a topic of conversation, I tried the strobe on the diary again. I should have asked Elizabeth first for the floor started to dissolve. We stepped back quickly as a large chamber appeared. I looked down. I wish I hadn't for I saw it was full of small white creatures who up to that point seemed to have been sleeping.

---~---

E.

Sometimes James impresses me with this heroic deeds and other times he does not quite meet my expectations. That is the way of men I believe and I have no quarrel with it. However there are also times when he performs inexplicable feats devoid of all sensible reason. His application of the strobe in the keep was one of these.

At first I thought I was looking into some charnel house or a vision from Dante or Bosch. There were hundreds of them pressed together in sleep or death, none bigger than two or three feet. Imperceptibly at first they began to rise out of the pit. They floated upwards towards us, turning and tumbling over and over. And then.... they awoke.

Pandemonium ensued, not least within my mind, as these creatures writhed in panic trying to grasp anything that they could as they rose up through the chamber and out through the windows and doors. Some had wings.

"My God, James! What have you done! You have unleashed the demons of Hell."

---~---

J.

What had I done? Had I really opened the gates of Hell? It truly was a vision of that other place buried deep in my psyche. They were struggling to keep still, grabbing anything they could as they rose through the air. Those that failed drifted helplessly out of the windows and gaps in the ruins and up into the sky. Others were crawling slowly up the steps. I suddenly realised they were trying get to the capsule. My God, they must be Martians. How long had they been here? Some held on but others drifted off. Gravity seemed to have no influence on them. Like Wells in Rievaulx they seemed to be trying to keep in time and space.

They did not notice us at first but then I realised we were almost transparent. I had to find out what they were doing. Elizabeth was trying to drag me out but I couldn't leave. I grabbed her hand and pulled her unwillingly up those steps again.

There were by now dozens of them on the stairs. They were weak creatures. Their skin pale white and smooth brushed against me and a single touch would send them off into the air. I had the distinct impression that they had a third leg which they used to propel themselves. When we arrived at the capsule we saw that a small aperture had opened and the creatures were scrambling inside. Were they trying to escape? Against all reason I peered inside. There must have been already a dozen of them in there struggling to reach and hold levers and dials. Two globes hung in the middle of the room, each like the one in the Control Room at Midhurst which I immediately recognised as Earth and Mars.

Then they noticed me.

Faint sounds like mosquitos buzzing in your ear at night

entered my mind. One of the creatures came near me. It was only about three feet tall and very thin. I could see that the whiteness was in fact an almost transparent gossamer suit which encased its body. It was disconcertingly familiar like a character from Lewis Carroll. The head was like that of a cat but its ears were more like a rabbit's which twitched and rotated like antennas. Its eyes were wide set and bulged and blinked like a frog's and in between there seemed to be a small opaque disc recessed into the forehead like the remains of a third eye. What I thought was a third leg was actually a thick tail like a kangaroo's on which it rested its body. I involuntarily moved back but found myself pressed against the wall. I could feel its hands touching me. They were very human with four fingers and an opposing thumb but without nails. They moved gently over my torso. It was searching me! I looked at its face. The small disc or eye seemed to grow larger. God, it was searching my mind as well as my body. I could hear the mosquito like sound moving in my mind. I suddenly realised what it wanted. It was after the diary!

I looked for an escape. The door was barely six feet away. I made sure I had Elizabeth held tightly but just as tried to leave I saw or felt the alien's finger press against my head and an orange globe began to materialise in front of me. It grew larger and larger. Then I realised I was falling towards it. Faint lines and markings appeared which somehow looked familiar. It was Mars! Great ice tinged fissures punctuated the desert landscape and here and there rows of vents rose like termite hills from the ground, spewing dark clouds of gas linked by networks of roads or tubes.

The planet rushed up towards me then I felt a shift in direction and we were skimming across the surface. Suddenly the land opened up and we descended into one of the great fissures. Clouds rose from the dry ice capped ridges warmed by the weak sunlight. Deimos or Phobos hung in the sky and at the end of the valley near the horizon, a tiny white-yellow sun. Then down we fell again at an incredible speed. I thought we were going to crash. But at the last moment the ground became transparent and we dived into a 3D world of caverns and chambers full of great ships and machinery. Thousands of the creatures were busy working. I realised I was watching the construction of an invasion force.

As I floated through a vast network of tubes and tunnels, that familiarity of the landscape I had felt when I approached the planet jogged my memory and I remembered those early drawings of the canals of Mars first seen by astronomers in the 1870s and which by the early twentieth century had mysteriously vanished. I had made copies as a child which I had kept on the wall in my bedroom while I absorbed the Martian stories of Heinlein and Burroughs. When I was older I was disappointed to find that later astronomers had put these canals down to an optical illusion or aberration in the lenses of Victorian telescopes. Now I realised, with not a little satisfaction, that what the nineteenth century astronomers had seen was real. Perhaps a great Martian storm had buried them underground or perhaps the Martians had detected our observations and covered them. Only the vents from their factories were still visible which scientists in my time before the invasion had thought were pockets of frozen carbon dioxide turning to gas in the warmth of the weak sun and bursting through the surface.

I had been travelling in this Martian mindscape for miles. I could not understand why they were showing me their preparations until I realised that in searching my mind they had inadvertently let me into theirs. This realisation was immediately felt by the Martian and I found myself flying back out into space like a film in reverse. The buzzing sound in my head stopped and the vision vanished.

I was back in the Keep.

I looked down. There were now three of the creatures in front of me. Their hands were outstretched. They were still in my brain and I could feel myself wanting to give them the diary.

Suddenly I realised why they wanted it. It was a spy. They had used it to gather information on our world for their invasion and they wanted it back.

But I knew if we gave it to them they would know the outcome of the invasion and the bacteria that would destroy them.

My hand was reaching for the diary in my pocket but as I grasped it I heard a familiar voice calling faintly from the back of mind.

"James! James! Can you hear me? Don't give them the diary!"

Against my will my hand was slowly drawing the diary out of my pocket. For some reason a vaguely familiar aroma of musk and oranges percolated through my mind. I felt myself weakening, drifting away from the Martians. Then, a soft gentle moist tongue pressed against my ear. My hand relaxed its grip. Elizabeth came into view.

"James! Oh you are there. I saw everything - we must flee."

I didn't need to be told twice.

We ran out into the courtyard. Creatures were still floating up into the sky frantically trying to grab something. Others were clinging to walls and trees. They made no attempt to stop us.

"We must destroy it, James."

"We'll be stuck here."

"My time is not a bad place to live, James."

"Elizabeth, I've read about your medicine, surgical tools and as for anaesthetics, well, I'm too much of a coward. We must get out of here. These creatures unless they have some magic weaponry are too fragile to stop us."

It was almost pitch black but there was still light enough to make out the people whom we had seen earlier by the gate. They were standing motionless in shock. I realised what they were seeing: one lady in green and hundreds of pixies dancing about; the legend being created right in front of them.

As we approached the gate, they ran off, shrieking.

---~---

E

I had never run so fast in my life. The creatures were everywhere but as James said they did not bother us though his demonstration of their weakness by kicking one that had clung to my skirts high into the air was rather unsporting. I would have felt sorry for it if I had not witnessed their invasion.

By now it was so dark that we could not see the path to Helmsley. I said to James "We need a lantern otherwise we will break our necks or worse. Let us ask those people there."

We walked up to them. They were by the gatehouse still transfixed but when they saw us the ladies in the party screamed and they all ran off. We were left alone in the dark. Except of course for the Martians who thankfully were no longer in view but I could not help darting my eyes this way and that for their presence. I turned to James to make sure he was close by; as I did so a bright incandescent light shone from his hand. He saw my expression.

"Don't worry, Elizabeth. This time I have brought a torch." I could see he was quite proud of this and I encouraged it with a heartfelt hug and kiss for I could see by its light that the adventure, or should I say, our journey into hell, had taken much out of him.

A welcoming beam of light now shone ahead of us down the path to Helmsley and we ran back along the road as fast as we could to the Black Swan like two small children caught in the dark.

We needed help. This was getting too complicated. Every turn became a new adventure and dragged us deeper into a maze from which it seemed we could not escape.

And when we arrived much relieved in the village square, there was help, or so I hoped, waiting for us by the front door of the Inn.

---∼---

Out of Time

Chapter Seventeen

J.

"So", said Wells, as we sat down to eat a delicious steak and kidney pie at his expense. "You have seen the Martians."

We told him our story starting with the electronic diary he had given us.

He sat back and folded his hands. More beer arrived. My poor brain was in need of topping up. Then he leaned forward and said, "This is what I've gleaned."

"The first thing you have to realise is that we have been manipulated by the Martians for over a hundred years to prepare us for their invasion."

We looked stunned. I said, "Do you mean we've been ruled by Martians? I've often wondered where we got some of our politicians from."

"No, Mr Urquhart. Sadly they come from our own species. Somehow the Martians came into contact with Mr. Batalia whom they had identified as quite a genius in relativistic physics and neural nets and either gave him the diary or perhaps they just left it in a place where he would find it. It wasn't an ordinary diary, as you know. It showed him how to access the Dark Net which they had created."

"The Martians created the Dark Net?"

"Yes. As far as I can understand, it is not part of this world and the conduits to it pass through time as well as space. That's why no one has been able to penetrate it."

"And what about ComsMesh?"

"The Dark Net is connected to ComsMesh which is on Mars. I don't think Marco and his Staff at the Weber Institute knew that."

"I don't think anyone else did either", I said.

"Quite right, Mr Urquhart. They presumed they had invented it and everything they controlled was kept on the storage devices at Midhurst. But they were connected by a Dark Net conduit to Mars."

"So the Martians had access to all the human social media."

"Only those humans who used social media."

"But they would be the easiest to influence."

"Yes. Their plan was to get the human race in a semi-unconscious state, docile and compliant, to ease the invasion. They had seen how easily we were manipulated by simple advertising. They were very close to succeeding when you two turned up. Mr. Batalia could see the consequences of your actions and tried to put everything back but as you know he failed."

"So he must have been working for the Martians?"

"I don't think so. I think he genuinely thought he was trying to save the world from destroying itself through what he thought was his own social engineering programme. The Martians however were on a different schedule and expected the world to be asleep. But unfortunately for them we were still half awake."

"So when they arrived we were able to defend ourselves. And Porton Down came up with the goods once they knew how they ticked."

"But James, we shut down the computers at St. Anne's Hill. Surely that would have cut them off."

"Exactly, Mrs Urquhart, and do have some more pie. It was that event which caused them to start the invasion. They didn't know what we were doing so they had to attack."

"But here. I mean in the 1890s they don't know that yet." I said.

Elizabeth reached for my hand "But James they do! They have been in our minds. They not only now know we are aware of their preparations for invasion they also possibly know what happened to their invasion."

"Jeez. You're right Elizabeth. If they tell Mars then they might invade now when our weaponry is just sticks and stones. There aren't any planes, missiles, radio or even radar! We're f....."

There was a sudden rumble of thunder. I looked out of the window. It was a clear dark sky.

"That will be the ship leaving Earth for Mars", said Wells.

"Oh my God, James. What can we do?"

I realised now that poor Captain Intrepid had come to the end of his tether. Even his box of stupid ideas was empty.

Then there was another roll of thunder. This time much louder which rattled the windows. We ran to the door and were treated to a fantastic display of fireworks.

"Their ship has blown up!"

"They must have panicked and lost control."

"Or maybe those who did know how to control it floated away leaving just the Adminstaff to fly the ship."

"Actually", said Wells, "it was much simpler. That ship has been there since before the castle was built. The Normans built their Keep around it and used it as part of the structure. Must have been quite a surprise when they tried to take off."

"That would explain in my time why half the Keep is missing", I said. Then Captain Intrepid woke up.

"By the way, Wells, how do you know all this? And more importantly, how did we find you at Rievaulx?"

"I was wondering when you were going to ask that." He took a sip of his beer at the same time as I did. Elizabeth sat motionless. Then he continued. "I have found, Mr. Urquhart, that I am a man of exceptional moods. I do not know how far my experience is common. At times I suffer from the strangest sense of detachment from myself and the world about me; I seem to watch it all from the outside, from somewhere inconceivably remote, out of time, out of space, out of the stress and tragedy of it all. This feeling was very strong upon me that night when we met at Rievaulx."

I had a strong feeling as well because I remembered these were almost the exact words used by the unnamed hero in Wells' book, the War of the Worlds. It was one of my favourite passages. He continued.

"I thought I was asleep, dreaming. I found myself rising from my bed, out of my room. This had happened to me many times before. But this time the walls vanished and I was floating in a ruined cathedral which I later found out was Rievaulx Abbey. The floor was covered in what I at first thought were gravestones. But as I drew nearer I realised they were tombs or capsules. There was a transparency about them for within each I could just discern a small creature. I could not resist touching one of the tombs and to my horror the grey cover melted and the creature within stirred and opened its eyes. I was transfixed as it raised a limb and pressed a finger immediately to my head. Then, like you, I saw Mars. But at first a different Mars. A young planet, green and violet. A great ice ocean covered the northern hemisphere. From it lines or tubes radiated to the south connecting the myriads of craters where within each one I could see great artificial structures. Then it changed. Slowly the ice sea receded. Deserts formed. Great dust storms traversed the planet. The tubes disappeared into the ground and the structures in the craters became smaller until they also disappeared below the surface."

"The Martians must have seen that coming for hundreds or thousands of years", I said, "and made plans to go underground. I've got to hand it to them. Scientists are screaming at our politicians that we are destroying our world but no one will do anything. It's like when a fire alarm goes off. No one moves until they see the fire. But by then it is too late."

Elizabeth interjected. "Have you brought me to a world which is going to die, James?"

"Not as quickly as if you Victorians had continued to pollute the world."

"So, James, if we hadn't developed our science and industry, you would not have developed the means to control it."

I remembered just in time that women should be allowed the last word in an argument. If a man has the last word it's the start of a new argument. I continued.

"Anyway, back on Mars. If the atmosphere was thinning any residual water would boil off. Perhaps the receding of the ice sheets you saw was because the Martians were taking it beneath to store. Certainly a lot of our scientists are becoming convinced that there is a vast amount of salt water below the surface of Mars. Perhaps the Martians like their water salty."

"Quite so, Mr Urquhart. But what concerned me was a vision of the Earth from Mars. I could see the great blue oceans. Perhaps you are right and they are salt water creatures for much of the vision was of our watery surfaces. While I watched I wondered whether they had visited the Earth already and as if I commanded it I was on Earth. A great tripod loomed above me. There were others in the distance. Then I felt it probing my mind. It discovered I knew about the time machine and meeting Mr Batalia and how he built it. Then just as I felt it was about to probe deeper, thank God, you appeared. Using all my will I rose from the tomb and tried to warn you but, how can I say this delicately, you were too engrossed in each other. So I left you a message."

We sat back silent. Elizabeth was the first to speak.

---~---

E.

I had listened to Wells with fascination but something of importance concerned me which needed explanation if my philosophy of life was not to collapse. I turned to James for support.

"As you know, James, I have been brought up with religion. Not the dogmatic kind but that of the Church of England which has allowed a certain laissez faire or freedom in one's beliefs. It does not demand much except regular attendance at its functions and feasts. It is part of our society and, if I may suggest, quite secular in many ways, though I would not express that view in certain circles. But its philosophy has always allowed the freedom of will and encouraged individual responsibility. It does not insist that life is preordained."

"Where you going with this, Elizabeth?"

I had to try harder.

"Bear with me, James, for it is important. After listening to Mr Wells and looking back at all our exploits since we first met at Hamgreen, it is difficult not to believe that whatever decision we made was the only decision we were allowed to take. But if this is true then it questions our whole existence and what or why we are here."

"So you think that everything we have done was preordained?"

"I do not know, James. But it is difficult not to reach that conclusion."

"Well, my interpretation is a little more optimistic. I think, as you say, that if you take into account all the decisions we could have made compared to the ones we took, it does seem highly improbable we arrived where we are without some help. But I think this is where the Blind Watch Maker comes into play."

"The what?" For James was leaving me behind again.

"A watch or clock, in order to exist, can only be assembled in a certain way. A blind man given the parts of a watch will try thousands of different ways to construct it but only one method which requires the right parts in the right order will make the clock work."

"So, James, in order to be where or when we are, although there were hundreds of different decisions we only took the ones that brought us here. Any other decisions and we wouldn't be here. We have been very lucky blind watchmakers."

"No, Elizabeth. It's not luck. We are here because we are here. But remember a lot of decisions weren't critical. We could have gone to Rievaulx by the diary rather than by plane, train, dog cart and horse. I could have forgotten my torch. The Martian ship would have blown up whether I looked in the capsule or not."

"We could have forgotten to bring a change of clothes." I said.

"But from our experiences there was a high probability we would make that right decision."

"Maybe I do feel a little less convinced that we had no free will, James. I suppose the real test is now how do we get back. Will we make the right decisions?"

"Maybe it's impossible to get back."

"If that's the case I would look after you, James, in the same way you looked after me."

---~---

J.

There were a lot of attractions about living in the late Victorian and Edwardian period. I would see the Belle Epoch and Art Nouveau. I would fill our house with Arts & Crafts. However to take advantage of it I felt I would have to be reasonably wealthy. Mind you, I could mop up by publishing Einstein's theories of relativity before him. I imagined it: James Urquhart's Theories of Time and Space. I was away with the fairies - until an image arose of our children being called up in the First World War.

"Thank you, Elizabeth. I know you will look after me. But how long could we prevent ourselves from not trying to help people avoid the future? You know, such as the Boer War or even the First World War."

Wells interrupted. "What happens in this first world war, Mr. Urquhart?"

How could I tell him that in my world his son would be killed and he would spend many years at séances trying to contact him?

I kept my reply simple and change the subject. "Like all wars a lot of people will die who didn't want to die. But, Wells, do you have any idea how we can get back to my time?"

"You still have the diary. You could try it again." He said with a smile.

Elizabeth and I looked at each other. I could see she was expecting another decision. I took out the strobe and pressed the button.

---∼---

E.

I opened my eyes. We were still here. Mr Wells was looking at us quizzically.

"Nothing has happened, James."

"I think the battery is flat." He said.

"Do you have another, James?"

"No I don't. Perhaps you have some spare batteries in one of those FIVE bags you brought with you."

His look suggested that this was one of those occasions

when one's offer of assistance is not met with the gratitude it deserves and that any teasing would not be met with his usual humour. However, I felt that this was not the time to kowtow despite the risk. I persevered.

"What about the battery in your flash light? Would that not work?"

"Yes, it would." There was now a tinge of gratefulness in his expression which I knew had to be exploited quickly.

"James. You can't remember everything. Imagine if you had not brought a torch or change of clothes".

He removed the battery from his flash light and placed it in the strobe. He held my hand and pressed the button.

Still nothing. James was looking quite angry now. I thought it best to keep quiet. Then he said.

"Right, Elizabeth. I've had enough of this bloody adventure. I'm taking you home. And before you ask, Captain Intrepid is not getting a look in."

I was I admit a little afraid. "I'm sorry, James, if I......"

But before I could finish he turned to Mr Wells and said with much emphasis.

"Can you do anything to help us, Mr Wells? You seemed to have damn well 'helped' us with everything else."

---~---

J.

Wells was looking too comfortable considering our plight. What Elizabeth had said about how we were making decisions struck a chord. It was time for a little interrogation.

"This is the year you publish your Time Machine, isn't it?"

"Yes, Mr Urquhart, and I'm pleased to say it has proved very popular."

"And from what I can remember you describe a four-dimensional universe in which the fourth is time. Something that didn't really get accepted until Einstein about ten years from now."

"Yes, but as you know scientist have been producing papers on the four dimensions since the 1880s. It is nothing new. Newcomb and Hinton have done some excellent work on this."

"But if I remember correctly they were talking in four spatial dimensions. I believe there was a letter published by an anonymous author who proposed that time itself was the fourth dimension. I think he or she called it time-space. Was that you?"

"It is something I believe in."

"I agree, Mr Wells, because you go to great lengths in your book, The Time Machine, about time being the fourth dimension but unlike Newcomb who you name in your story, you postulate that you can move up and down the time dimension. That's very brave of you to challenge an eminent scientist - unless you knew something that he didn't."

"He was so close. I thought he needed a little help."

"You thought he needed a little help! Interesting. Now let's look at something else: Elizabeth's conjecture is that there are too many coincidences, Mr Wells. You turn up in the cavern at Midhurst just when we get there. You manage to operate the time machine and take it to Hamgreen even though I had taken the control levers out. Then there you are again when we were transported to Rievaulx via the diary. And surprise, surprise, here you are waiting for us at the Black Swan when we returned from the Castle."

Wells said nothing but rocked slowly back and forth in his chair. He seemed to be smiling again. However, I was having some difficulty seeing the funny side.

"OK, since you won't answer that. How about your amazing 'predictions' about the future? Let's list some: the war between

Germany and Poland in 1940 and then between the USA and Japan; the use of atomic weapons which I believe in some circles led to the idea to develop an atomic bomb; predicting tanks in your book the Land Ironclads; and finally you gave yourself away when I asked you how you met us in the ruined abbey. Your reason was almost a verbatim copy of the 'unknown' hero in The War of the Worlds.

I believe you are a time traveller, Mr. Wells, and you have manipulated us from Day One to further your own aims. What do you say to that?"

--- ~ ---

E.

James had amazingly put together, through his knowledge of physics and Mr Wells' books, everything that was causing me concern. It all made sense though what sense it made I could not immediately calculate.

I could tell from Wells' relaxed manner that James' deductions were close to the mark. Then Wells spoke.

"Well deduced, Mr Urquhart. You are almost right. Yes, I do travel in time but not in my corporeal body. You may have noticed that apart from your travels in your time machine I have stayed in my time. And in case you're wondering I am physically here, I have travelled up here. I do not know why I find myself out of my body at times and why I see things which others don't. I have some control of where or when I go but it takes great energy. There seem to be many time dimensions because each time I visit the future the world I see is a little different. But there is one thing that is common and that is the Martian invasion and my aim was to stop it.

I could not tell people what I have seen for they would not believe me and so I hit on the idea of writing Science Romances. I have found people are very susceptible to ideas from fiction especially scientists. Were you not inspired to do physics because of your love of Science Romances or Science Fiction and Fantasy as you call it?"

James nodded then said rather grudgingly, "Yes, but no one believed your stories so how do you think they helped?"

"I gave people dreams which through experimentation became reality. You went to the moon, made atomics, guided rockets, air ships and death rays. I gave you the ideas which would eventually make you sophisticated enough to defeat the Martians."

A thought came to me. I said, "Have you travelled to the past, Mr Wells?"

"I'm not aware of having done that, Mrs Urquhart. Perhaps the past is more fixed in time than the future. A change to the past could generate a thousand different futures and the power required to change time-space could be enormous."

'That could explain the power needed for Marco's time machine." Said James.

"I viewed his machine as extremely dangerous, Mr Urquhart. Just going to the past could destroy all our futures."

"We call that the butterfly effect. You travel to the distant past, tread on a butterfly and that insignificant action is magnified over millions of years."

"So, James, each trip to the past has changed our future a little." I said. "That could explain why we are not comfortable in the world to which we returned in your time."

"So why didn't you tell us what you were trying to do?"

"For precisely that reason, Mr Urquhart. That knowledge could have led you to different decisions."

I felt slightly overwhelmed with Wells' story; James and I had been used.

Then James got to the root of this enigma.

"Why did you choose us, Mr Wells, to save the world? I'm

just a simple scientist and Elizabeth is an unemployed lady of leisure?"

I thought this was a little unfair. I had worked very hard at my education and in many areas excelled James by a good mile.

"I didn't. Your meeting was by chance brought on by a distortion in time-space. You were unique. Unlike me, both of you could actually bodily travel through time."

"I don't like being used, Wells." Said James rather forcefully.

"Do you like your wife, Mr Urquhart? Surely you do not regret the phenomena that brought you together?"

James looked at me and then turned back to Wells. His shoulders slumped. I could see poor James was near the end of his tether.

"How do we get home, Mr Wells? We are very tired."

Wells came over to us and took the electric diary. He pressed a point on the back. Our surrounds blurred. I feared too late we were to be 'used' again.

---~---

E.

I opened my eyes expecting some new adventure. Instead I found us both in James' attic. The relief made me almost faint. I turned to James. He looked shattered. No doubt I did not look much better. We held each other tight for some time in silence. And then I noticed on James' desk amongst the wires and notes our original diaries. Wells somehow must have retrieved them or made facsimiles.

I opened mine and to my surprise found all our adventures recorded since we had given them to Wells and in my copperplate!

"What shall we do with these, James?"

"We will write a book."

For some reason, my clothing felt very tight. I looked down to adjust my skirts and noticed my waist was larger than it had been. I did not think that was the result of the game pie at the Black Swan.

"James?"

"Yes, Elizabeth?"

"I think I am with child!"

"What?" Then he looked at my figure. "Good god, so you are! We've only been, well you know, for about a month."

I could not explain it for I had known no other man except James for some years. But I realised with my reputation much depended on his faith in me. Just then I heard Jill coming up the ladder.

"Are you two back again? That's six months you've been away. What have you been doing this time?"

"Oh", she said regarding my form. "Well, er, congratulations. Would you like a cup of tea and tell me about the other things you've been doing?"

I turned to James who looked thankfully very pleased.

It was time to risk a tease. "Well, James, I trust next time I advise you not to look out of a train window you will remember the consequences."

---∼---

The End

Out of Time

Other Books by Bruce Macfarlane

from the
Time Travel Diaries of James Urquhart and Elizabeth Bicester

Book 1 Out of Time
The first diaries of the humorous and sometimes romantic time travel adventures of James Urquhart, minor science lecturer living in 2015 and Elizabeth Bicester, lady of leisure, whom he stumbles upon at a cricket match at Hamgreen in 1873. Despite their banter regarding each other's manners they manage through incredible feats of illogical deduction and with not a little help from James Maxwell, H. G. Wells, the Martians and some strange time devices, to save the world.

Book 2 A Drift Out of Time
In this volume, they have returned home to find they are not only in an alternative future but a different aspect of themselves. To get back to their world they must travel between Mars and Earth, drifting across time and space, until eventually they reach home and discover who the Martians really are.

Book 3 A House Out of Time
Once again, the intrepid couple have "retired' to a quiet life of ease in an alternative world after helping the Martians save the Earth and their own planet. Unfortunately, Elizabeth thought it would be a good idea to visit her ancestral home at Hamgreen to see what had become of it.
….Such is the curiosity of women.

Book 4 The Space Between Time
In these extracts from the Time Travel Diaries we find the intrepid couple enjoying a peaceful and romantic picnic by the

River Rother when a motor launch turns up complete with Mr Wells.

Apparently, a certain Mr Tesla has conducted one of his electro-magnetic experiments which has fractured time and dumped everyone in an alternative world of 1895. The problem is that only a few people have noticed the difference.

Mr Wells wondered if James and Elizabeth would like to help.

Short Stories
The Webs of Time

Here are seven short stories from the time travel diaries of James Urquhart, minor scientist, who lived in 2015 and Elizabeth Bicester whom he met at cricket match in 1873.

They are narrated by Professor Rolleston who discovered the original diaries and who spent his life, when not hunting fairies, trying to understand their contents and the reasons for their existence.

Three of the stories, Northern Nights, A Holiday in Cornwall and the Haunted Mill, previously appeared in Three Tales Out of Time.

Notes on Arthurian Literature.

This book contains my notes on Arthurian literature examine the origins of Arthur and the historical events associated with him.

It also reviews the Celtic origins of the Grail stories and the significance of their appearance at the time of the crusades after the fall of Jerusalem in 1009 and recapture by Godfrei de Boullion in 1099 and their re-emergence in Mallory's Mort D'Arthur after the fall of Constantinople in 1454.

Subjects covered in the book are;
The Origins of Arthur.
Possible Links to Historical Events.
Problems with Dating Events in the 5th and 6th Centuries.
Climatic and Astronomical Phenomenon in 5th and 6th Century Britain.
The Appearance of the Grail Stories.
Historical Characters and Events in the Grail Stories.
Celtic and Other Origins of the Grail and the Grail Characters.
Malory and the Tales of King Arthur.

About the Author

Bruce is a retired Health Physicist who lives with his wife on the south coast of England, just a few minutes' walk from the sea. When he's not researching King Arthur, he's out walking on the South Downs with his wife and his friends trying to remember all the names of the flowers and mushrooms his wife has identified.

When it's raining he can be found sometimes in his "shed" as his wife calls it, trying to master new jazz chords.

A life of writing scientific reports and reading early science fiction, especially the genre of time travel such as the works of Anderson, Simak and Wells encouraged him to start writing his own novels about the adventures of a modern man and a Victorian lady whom he met at a cricket match in 1873.

His stories have been described as "Tom Holt meets P.G. Wodehouse meets Philip K. Dick meets Fortean Times."

You can get more information on this and his other books and hobbies at: his blog at:

timediaries.wordpress.com

Or you can visit our website at:

www.aldwickpublishing.com/

June 2019

Printed in Great Britain
by Amazon